The Artificial Grandma

YEARLING BOOKS/YOUNG YEARLINGS/YEARLING
CLASSICS are designed especially to entertain and
enlighten young people. Patricia Reilly Giff, consultant
to this series, received the bachelor's degree from
Marymount College. She holds the master's degree in
history from St. John's University, and a Professional
Diploma in Reading from Hofstra University. She was
a teacher and reading consultant for many years, and
is the author of numerous books for young readers.

For a complete listing of all Yearling titles, write to
Dell Readers Service, P.O. Box 1045,
South Holland, IL 60473.

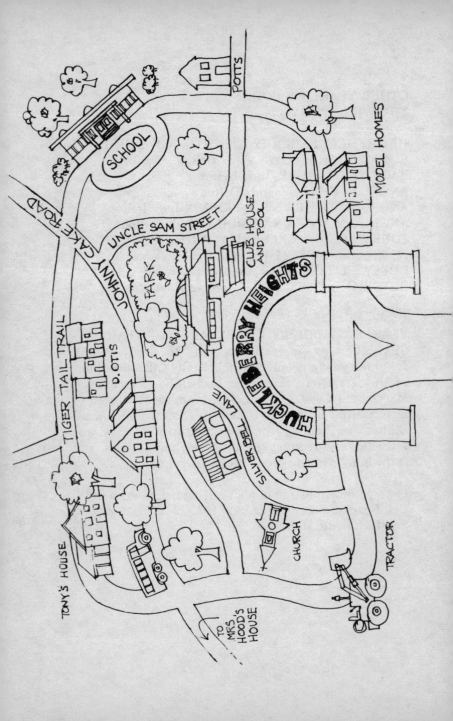

The Artificial Grandma

Judy Delton

Illustrated by Alan Tiegreen

A YEARLING BOOK

Published by
Dell Publishing
a division of
Bantam Doubleday Dell Publishing Group, Inc.
666 Fifth Avenue
New York, New York 10103

ISBN: 0-440-40315-4

Printed in the United States of America

August 1990

10 9 8 7 6 5 4 3 2 1

CWO

*FOR CAROLE NELSON DOUGLAS, WHO DIDN'T
NEED MY CLASS TO SUCCEED*

And with thanks to Lori Mack, editor

1

*A*nthony *Doyle, age ten,* I wrote in the wet cement in our new driveway. Then I put my hand down beside it so I would be preserved forever.

"When I'm really old like eighteen I'll look back and think what a little kid I was," I said to Edgar Allan Potts, my best friend in Huckleberry Heights.

"When you're about eighty like Mrs. Hood," said Gus, my eight-year-old brother, "you probably won't be able to read it."

Mrs. Hood lived in an old house on the edge of Huckleberry Heights. When they put in the condos, she wouldn't move.

"And then you'll be dead and somebody else will live here in your house and they'll say, 'I wonder who Tony Doyle was?' " said Edgar.

I suppose he was right. Cement lasts a long time. In the museum in St. Paul there are these statues and rocks that were made about the year one. All the people died but that stuff is still here.

"This is an important moment," said Gus solemnly. He stuck his hand in the cement too. Then he printed FERGUS DOYLE, AGE EIGHT, next to it.

"This stuff sticks to your hands," said Gus. We had a hard time getting it off.

"Let's sit on the steps and watch your name get hard," said Edgar.

We sat and sat in the hot sun. It was the middle of summer, and Minnesota summers are scorchers. Every once in a

2

ANTHONY
DOYLE
age 10

while Gus tried the cement, but it was still soft.

Lenny Fox, Gus's friend, came along on his bike. He sat down with us to watch the cement get hard.

We all lived in condominiums in Huckleberry Heights. That's a suburb of St. Paul. We used to live in the city, but my mom wanted a yard and fresh air and a barbecue and a tree, so we moved.

Condos are just like real houses except that they are attached to one another. Like four houses in one big house. We live on Tiger Tail Trail. Lenny and Edgar live about a block away. In fall we will be going to a brand-new school. They are building it right now. The clubhouse is already finished, and it's got a swimming pool we can swim in, even in winter.

I have a sister named Marcy and a sheepdog named Smiley. Marcy's twelve, and Smiley's six months. He's the son of Lenny's dog, Gladys.

As we sat there watching the cement, a car drove up. A lady with a big bag of stuff got out and looked at the street address.

"Is this number sixteen Tiger Tail Trail?" she asked.

I pointed. Number 16 is right next to us. We are at number 15.

"I'm looking for Bud and Jennie Ray," she said.

"They are our neighbors. They just moved in last month," I said.

"That's the Welcome Wagon lady," whispered Lenny. "She came when we moved in and we were supposed to get all these gifts and all we got was coupons."

"They told us it was like a party," said Gus. "But it wasn't. There was no party, and no presents."

"There wasn't even a wagon," said Edgar. "No wagon, no welcome."

The lady knocked on the Rays' door, and Jennie let her in. We went back to watching the cement.

5

Way down Tiger Tail Trail I could see my mom's car turn in. She drove through the HUCKLEBERRY HEIGHTS arch beneath a sign that said CONDOS FOR SALE. LOW DOWN PAYMENT TO QUALIFIED BUYERS. Then she parked in front of the house because the cement in the driveway was wet.

When she got out of the car, she took the mail out of the box and stood admiring the driveway. "Be sure to keep Smiley off it," she called to us. "We don't want paw prints all over it." She didn't notice our paw prints, I guess.

My mom works in St. Paul. She owns her own faucet company. She loves faucets. Not just regular old chrome faucets—hers come in silver, goldtone, porcelain, bronze, and pewter. The name of the company is Trixie's Taps. (That's her name, Trixie.)

"I was at a community meeting this afternoon," said my mother. "At the clubhouse. I have some very exciting news. I'll tell you about it at a family meeting tonight." She walked up the steps and ruffled my hair with her hand.

We hated meetings with my mom. They are a big thing with her and the outcome is usually some disaster. Last time she made us go to school in June. She hates to see us with time on our hands.

"Idle hands are the devil's workshop," she often tells us. We should have looked busier when she drove up.

"Did you hear?" asked Marcy, sticking her head out of her bedroom window. "A family meeting. Mom has some news. Whatever it is it isn't my fault."

Edgar and Lenny looked uneasy. Last time, they got trapped into our mother's meeting. Now they waved good-bye and left before it happened again.

Gus and I set the chairs up for the meeting. The three of us lined up in the front row. Smiley sat on the end. I was hoping if she saw us all ready, she'd get it over with before dinner. None of us could eat anyway, wondering what the news was.

"Good," she said, coming down the steps with some papers in her hand. I knew it couldn't be report cards. This was summer.

Marcy read the minutes of the last meeting. "It was moved and seconded that we let Mom make us go to summer classes at the clubhouse," she finished.

My mom frowned at the wording of that sentence, but went on.

"This meeting is good news," she said.

Define *good news*, I thought. She thought summer school was good news.

"Huckleberry Heights has been chosen as one of the four suburbs to participate in a pilot program for the month of August."

We didn't move. We were waiting for the other shoe to drop. So far, so good. But what kind of program?

8

"The idea is to put senior citizens from the city in contact with families in the suburbs. Families with children."

"Why?" asked Gus.

"That's a good question, Fergus," said my mother. "The senior citizens that sign up live in St. Paul and have no families nearby and no grandchildren to enjoy. They would like to be with children, and they would like to get out of the hot city to a place with back-yards. It would be like a vacation for them, and for the families who take them in. And children like you would have a sort of foster grandparent."

I heard the other shoe drop.

"Huckleberry Heights is lucky enough to welcome four of these senior citi-zens. The community is now looking for suitable families who wish to open their homes and their hearts to one of them."

I had the picture. We were going to have an artificial grandma.

"We already have grandparents," said Marcy. "We don't need more."

"Not *need*, Marcella. *Want*. And our own are in Nevada," she responded. "We hardly ever see them. And your father's parents are in Florida. We never go as far as Florida."

My dad lived in California.

"I thought it would be a good thing to take one of these people into our home for the month. They would just be part of the family and do what we do. What do you think?"

My mom is a pushover when it comes to community service. She even taught acting this summer, and she doesn't know a thing about it. Well, she does have a flair for the dramatic, but she isn't a teacher or anything.

"I want one," said Gus.

Leave it to Gus to make a snap judgment.

"Where would this grandparent sleep?" said Marcy suspiciously.

"Your rooms are big," said my mother. "We could put a cot in any one of them."

It sounded like my mom's mind was made up. "And now if someone will move that we adjourn our meeting, we can have our dinner," she said.

"Ho ho ho no," I said. "We haven't voted yet."

That was just like my mother. Sneak by without a vote and move on to dinner because she knows Gus will say anything to get food.

"Well, I thought I'd check on the details before we vote," said my mother.

You may think that is perfectly reasonable, but I tell you this: We will never get to vote. By the time we turn around, a stranger will be sitting on our couch with a shawl on and the heat turned up to ninety and it will be too late to do a thing.

But Gus had already said, "I move that we adjourn this dumb meeting and eat." Marcy seconded the motion.

12

"It has been moved and seconded that we adjourn," said my mom.

The die was cast. I was doomed to be the grandchild of an artificial grandparent.

2

"Why can't Mom leave our summers alone?" said Marcy when my mom left the room. "Now that the classes are over I thought we could do what we want."

I secretly looked forward to this artificial grandparent. We never had a grandma or grandpa around to come to our birthday parties. Just my aunt Fluffy, who is my mom's sister. We could use a bigger family.

"He'll just do his own thing, like Mom

14

said," I told Marcy. "It's not as though we have to entertain him or anything. Maybe he will make cookies or vacuum or play the piano or something."

"We don't have a piano," said Gus.

"Well, a fiddle, then. Maybe he will play a guitar."

After dinner I said, "Will we get a man or a woman?" to my mom.

"There are two men and two women," she said. "We will have to see which one is suitable for us. It's like adoption, you don't know which till it arrives."

"Are we going to send out announcements?" asked Marcy. "Like 'new arrival at our house, a bouncing baby grandpa, weight two hundred pounds'?"

Gus began to roar. "A bouncing baby grandpa!" he sang. "That's pretty funny."

I wondered if he'd still be laughing when this bundle of joy shared his room with him.

Not much happened about the program for a while and we thought maybe

15

Mom had forgotten "Project Grandpa." Gus and Lenny and Edgar and I watched the men putting up the new condos. We watched them pave the streets and pour cement and gravel.

"Are you getting a senior citizen in August?" I asked the other kids.

"My dad said we can't give them the attention they deserve," said Edgar.

"We applied too late," said Lenny. "They were all gone. I think they should have more than four."

"I wouldn't want no old lady living with me," said Punkin Head Maloney, chewing on a bologna sandwich even though it was only ten o'clock in the morning. Punkin Head is in Gus's class because he flunked kindergarten.

"Lily is getting one," said Edgar.

Lily is in my class. She likes me. Maybe a grandparent would keep her out of my hair for August. Maybe she and this grandma would go shopping at the mall and Lily wouldn't hang on me all the time.

When we got home, there was a note on the refrigerator. It said, *Feed Smiley. Take out the trash. I've gone to get Hilary. Love, Mom. P.S. Set the cot up in Marcy's room.*

"What's a Hilary?" asked Gus.

"It's a name," I said. "I thought it was a man's name."

"It must be a grandma," said Marcy. "Because she's going to be in my room."

I'd been thinking about a grandpa for so long now, it was hard to change. An artificial grandma named Hilary?

Gus got out the vacuum cleaner, and I moved the little table up from the basement and put it in Marcy's room next to the cot. Marcy went out and picked some petunias from our garden, and we put them in a vase on the table.

"I think she should have my bed," said Marcy, "and I'll sleep on the cot."

I thought that was very generous of Marcy, considering she was the one who had to share and Gus and I got to keep our rooms to ourselves.

"It might be fun to have a roomie," said Daisy Otis, who had come over to meet Hilary. The Otises live next door. She's Marcy's friend. "I wish I had a brother or sister sometimes," Daisy went on.

"A grandma's not like no sister," said Punkin Head, who had come with Edgar and Lenny.

"I won't have much privacy," admitted Marcy. "And how can I have slumber parties?"

"She could come," said Daisy, who was checking Marcy's closet for new clothes. "Besides, it's only for August. When school starts, she'll be gone."

"My grandma's got false teeth," said Punkin Head. "She can take them in and out when she wants."

"Will she eat with you?" asked Edgar.

"No, she's going to eat with Smiley," I said sarcastically. "Of course she's going to eat with us. She's like one of the family."

I must have been nervous about Hilary's arrival, the way I snapped at my best friend.

We heard a car drive up in the driveway. Smiley barked. He must have been nervous too.

"They're here!" shouted Gus.

We all ran out in the front yard and stood around trying to look normal. A small crowd had gathered, a kind of welcoming committee. Jennie was there, and the Otises, and even some strangers.

My mom opened the car door and took a suitcase out of the backseat. Then she opened the other door and said, "Children, I'd like you to meet our guest, Hilary Hassleby."

Hilary climbed out of the car. She had a big smile on her face. It was a nice round friendly face. She walked right up to Edgar and threw her arms

around him and said, "You must be Anthony. I feel like I know you already."

"Thank you," said Edgar politely, "but I am Edgar Allan Potts."

Hilary must not have heard him because she was busy hugging Daisy Otis now. "And you must be Marcella!" she said.

Before she could mistake Lenny for Gus, my mom said, "No, these are my children over here."

Hilary said, "Dear me, I'm so sorry. I must be nervous from all the excitement."

Everyone stood in line to welcome Hilary and shake her hand, and when they left we all trooped into the house and Hilary opened her suitcase and took out a package for each of us. And it wasn't even anyone's birthday. Mine was a Parcheesi game, and Marcy got a bangle bracelet, and Gus got some Play-Doh.

"Thank you," said Marcy, giving Hilary a hug. Gus and I thanked her too, but I figured we didn't know her well enough to hug her yet.

My mom put out some fancy little sandwiches on her lead crystal plate that was too good for the dishwasher, and I was glad Punkin Head wasn't there or all the sandwiches would have been gone in one minute.

"We are so glad to have you here," my mother said. "And I want you to make yourself right at home."

We gave Hilary a tour of the house and showed her her room. She unpacked her things and said, "I love it here already! All the fresh air and open space and flowers and trees. What a fine place Huckleberry Heights is!"

"She's nice," Marcy whispered to me in the kitchen.

Hilary was nice. Very very nice. But I couldn't help wondering what she was going to do all day long.

That night Hilary came and tucked us all in and told us stories about her childhood. About growing up in Kansas on a farm and walking four miles to school every day. About Gypsies and the town dances and how her brother was mistaken for a chicken thief.

I couldn't wait till the next night to hear more.

In the morning I found out what she was going to do during the day. Lenny's father had planned to take us fishing. Marcy and Daisy were taking Gus to the dentist in Yankee Doodle Mall to get his teeth fluorided. Hilary looked so lonely, I said, "Would you like to come fishing with us?"

I thought she'd say, No, I have things to do right here, but she didn't.

"I love to!" she said. "I love to fish. Just let me get some food together, and I'll be ready."

"How come you asked her?" grumbled Punkin Head when he found out. "You and me and Lenny and Edgar are just right for those boats that hold five. What will we do with her?"

I looked at Hilary out in the backyard digging for worms. On the counter was a big basket with lunch she had packed for all of us.

"Look," I said. "Hilary packed us a great lunch."

Punkin Head lifted the corner of the cloth that covered the basket. There were chicken legs and potato salad and chocolate cupcakes.

"She made that this morning," I said.

Punkin Head rubbed his hand over his stomach. "We can always get another boat," he said.

When Lenny's dad came by with the car, I said, "Mr. Fox, this is Hilary Hassleby."

Hilary put the lunch basket over one arm and reached out her hand to shake his. "I love to fish!" she said. "It is very nice of you to let me come."

"Welcome aboard," said Mr. Fox. "The more the merrier."

Hilary and I and Punkin Head squeezed into the backseat with the food. Lenny held the can of worms up front. His dad's tackle box was on the floor. We drove up to Edgar's house and gave a toot and Edgar came running out with a fishing pole.

"It's a great day for fishing," said Mr. Fox.

"Perfect!" said Hilary. "The almanac says today is the day to fish."

Then Mr. Fox and Hilary began discussing full moons and zodiac signs and how dry it was. I tried to keep Punkin Head's fingers out of the lunch.

"How come your artificial grandma came along?" whispered Edgar.

"She likes to fish," I said. "She'd be lonely at home."

"She could do stuff with Marcy, and Daisy," said Lenny.

What was this? A conspiracy against my grandma?

"They took Gus to the dentist," I said.

Liberty Lake was just on the edge of Huckleberry Heights. When we got there,

26

the boat man was glad to rent us two boats instead of one.

"I say three in each boat will give us room to spread out," said Lenny's dad. "Should we draw straws for which boat we get?"

While we put on our life jackets, Mr. Fox wrote our names on an old envelope and tore them apart. I drew them out of Hilary's fishing hat, one at a time. Edgar and Lenny got Mr. Fox. Punkin Head and I got Hilary.

Hilary divided the lunch carefully, putting half into the other boat. The man helped us into our boats and we shoved off.

Hilary rowed until we came to some weeds. Lenny's dad was so far away, we could hardly see his boat. I wished we were all together. I missed Lenny and Edgar.

"Now we'll drop the anchor," said Hilary. "These weeds are where the smallmouth bass are. Bass make a good dinner."

I wondered if bass with small mouths tasted better than ones with big mouths.

Hilary seemed to know what she was talking about. We were lucky to have an expert in our boat.

"We'll get more fish than those guys!" said Punkin Head.

Hilary baited our hooks and fastened the bobbers on the lines.

"I'll just get you started," she said. "Then you can bait your own."

Hilary reached into her bag. "This is an inflatable raft," she said, pointing to a little folded-up package. "Just in case we need it, we press this little button here, and it will inflate."

"We can swim," I said.

"Good," said Hilary. "But a person can't be too safe. Just in case."

I put my feet up on the seat and leaned back against the lunch basket. I watched our bobbers move up and down on the sparkling water. We were lucky to live near such a pretty lake. A lake full of fish. A lake out in the country where the air was fresh and there was plenty of space. I stared at the clouds. One was shaped like a kangaroo. Another one looked like a baby grand piano. The piano and kangaroo collided and turned into a big horse.

Hilary told us stories of fishing with her father in Kansas. Stories of big fish that got away.

"I'm hungry," said Punkin Head.

"It's a little early for lunch," said Hilary. "But one cupcake won't hurt."

Punkin Head held his pole with one hand and a chocolate cupcake in the other.

Just when I wondered if Hilary was right about the bass weeds, I felt something pull on my line.

"Your bobber is down!" shouted Punkin Head with his mouth full of cake.

I reeled my line in. It felt like a huge

fish. It swam in circles, round and round, trying to get away. "Get the net!" I shouted.

But Hilary just laughed. "It's just a little sunny," she said.

I pulled it in, and it flashed in the sun. I caught the first fish! It looked huge to me! I couldn't wait to show it to the guys!

Hilary grabbed the line and wiggled the hook out of the fish's mouth. Then right before my eyes, she threw the fish back into the water, as far from the boat as she could.

"Grow up, little sunny!" she said. "Come back when you're a man!"

"My fish," I said.

"You'll get a big fish, Tony. That was just a baby. We have to throw those back. It's the law."

I never heard of that law. But maybe Hilary was right. My fish was really meant to be a bigger fish. I put a worm on my line and threw it back into the water.

In a little while Punkin Head's bobber went down into the water.

"Hey!" he called. "I've got a whale here!"

This time we knew it was a keeper. This thing was a giant. It bent Punkin Head's pole in half, it was so strong. This was one monster fish.

I got the net and held it out. Hilary guided the line into the boat. Punkin Head was sweating with excitement.

"Boy, look at this thing," he said.

I got the stringer ready, to put the fish on.

"Why has he got whiskers?" said Punkin Head as the huge fish flapped in the bottom of the boat.

"Those are not whiskers," said Hilary. "They are stingers. We have to be careful and wear a glove when we take him off the hook, or we will get stung."

Hilary put on a canvas glove and grabbed the fish. She had to use a little pliers to get the hook out of his mouth.

I held out the stringer. "Our first fish!" I said.

But Hilary shook her head. "Bullhead," she said tersely. "Bullheads are bad for the lakes. They eat all the baby walleyes and smallmouth bass and sunnys. Have to get rid of him."

We couldn't see what Hilary did with Punkin Head's fish, because she turned around with her back to us. But she didn't put it on the stringer where the savers go, and she didn't throw it back in the lake.

"I want my fish," wailed Punkin Head.

"No good," said Hilary. "You will catch a big smallmouth bass here in these weeds, Punkin Head. Fishing takes patience."

Punkin Head began to pout. He wasn't famous for his patience.

"I think it's time for lunch," said my artificial grandma.

Punkin Head's face changed so fast, it was like he forgot all about his fish. He grabbed the basket and passed it down to Hilary.

She put a red-and-white checked tablecloth over the empty seat in the boat, as if it were a little table. Then she put paper plates out and loaded them with chicken legs and potato salad and pickles and all the stuff Punkin Head loves. I love it too.

"It's just like a picnic," shouted Punkin Head.

Hilary gave us forks and paper napkins and little moist towelettes to wash the fish smell off our hands. I sat back and ate and listened to the water lap lap lap the side of the boat. I watched a mother duck and her little babies swimming along the shore. The sun felt really good on my bare arms and legs. Maybe I'd be a professional fisherman when I grew up. I could practically live in a boat out here.

I had another chicken leg and Punkin Head had two more, and just when I had almost fallen asleep, Hilary passed around the cupcakes with the fudge frosting hanging over the side all gooey and nice.

"Now!" said Hilary, clearing away the lunch things. "Let's catch some big fish for our supper."

"You bet!" said Punkin Head, baiting his hook. We threw our lines in again and watched our bobbers. We watched and watched our bobbers. It seemed like forever.

Finally, Hilary caught a long, shiny fish. We got excited all over again, but she muttered, "Carp," and threw it back.

"Why?" shouted Punkin Head.

"Wormy," said Hilary. "Carp are full of worms. Can't eat them."

After another hour Hilary pulled up the anchor and rowed us over to another spot. We pulled in a lot of little sunnies and crappies, and Hilary threw them back because they were too small.

Pretty soon I didn't even get excited when I caught one.

"I have to go to the bathroom," said Punkin Head.

"I guess we will call it a day," said Hilary.

It looked like Mr. Fox was thinking the same thing. Their boat was heading toward shore.

Coming home with no fish was humiliating. Even a leftover cupcake didn't cheer us up.

When we got to the dock, the boat rental man pulled us up and helped us out.

"Any luck?" Mr. Fox shouted.

We shook our heads. I carried in the empty stringer.

Then Lenny and Edgar crawled out of the boat. Edgar's glasses were all spotted with lake water. In his hand he carried a stringer too. But his was filled with fish. Small fish, but real fish. Fish flapping and sparkling.

Lenny and his dad had a pail. In the pail were more fish. Small fish, and one bullhead and one carp. And one small-mouth bass.

"Next time I'm going in your boat!" I said.

Mr. Fox laughed. "You should have fished in our spot," he said.

Hilary looked at their fish politely and didn't say a thing about their being small or wormy. "We'll have to come again real soon" was all she said.

Edgar and Lenny swung their fish as we walked. They made sure we saw them. They even brought them in the bathroom with them. "Hold these a minute," they said to Punkin Head and me.

They swung them as we walked to the car, pretending they were a lot heavier than they were. They moaned and groaned about it, as if we should offer to help carry the big catch.

In the car, Punkin Head whispered,

"If you didn't bring her along, we would have fish too."

"Hilary is nice," I whispered back. "If we didn't bring her, we wouldn't have had any lunch."

We stopped at an ice-cream stand and Hilary bought us a cold drink.

When we got home, my mom held out the frying pan as a kind of joke.

"The middle of the day isn't the best for fishing," said Hilary. "We'll have to get up early next time, or else go for the evening fishing."

"Edgar and Lenny got some," I said. "They're having them for supper."

Hilary bustled around the kitchen. "I'll make us a nice tuna fish salad," she said. "I'm so sorry Anthony and Punkin Head were disappointed. But tuna will be a nice supper."

I hate tuna.

My mom made some corn muffins to go with it, so it wasn't too bad.

"Some new people moved into Daisy's condo," said Marcy. "They have a boy named George. He's going into seventh grade."

"How nice, dear," said my mom, buttering a muffin. "Maybe you and Daisy can show him the neighborhood."

Gus reached down and gave Smiley a mound of tuna salad under the table. Smiley is supposed to be outside when we eat, but Gus lets him in.

"I have an idea," said Hilary. "Perhaps we can have a barbecue tomorrow night in the backyard and invite him and his family. Sort of a welcoming party."

"What a good idea," said my mom.

"I can make my famous barbecue sauce," said Hilary. "It will be my treat. I'll get the steaks and make a salad and we can put potatoes on the grill too."

"Can Daisy come?" asked Marcy.

"Of course," said Hilary. "The more the merrier."

After we cleared the table, Hilary went into the living room to make her list.

"Isn't that nice of Hilary?" said Marcy. "I mean, that's a great thing to do."

I had to agree. Hilary was awfully nice.

"Mom said Lenny and Edgar and Punkin Head can come too," said Gus, coming into the kitchen. "I'll go invite them."

"I'll hurry home from work," said my mom, "and bring the dessert."

Marcy went to invite Daisy and George and George's family, the Nelsons. When she got back, she said, "They can all come!"

The next morning when I woke up, the first thing I heard was a loud clap of thunder. Rain was beating on my window like a bunch of woodpeckers. Hilary was making pancakes downstairs. I could smell them.

"Sit down, Tony," she said when I came into the kitchen. She put a plate of pancakes in front of me, and some

41

warm maple syrup. "It's from my cousin in Vermont," she said. "He makes it himself."

Hilary took off her apron and said, "I'll just run to the mall and get the things for the barbecue now."

"It looks like it's going to rain all day," I said. A big black cloud hung over our house.

"It will clear in time for the barbecue," called Hilary as she went out the door with her umbrella. "The sun is trying to come out, I can see it."

Marcy came into the kitchen. "We are going to be rained out," she said. "And George is so cute. I think he likes me."

After breakfast I went over to Lenny's with Gus. We called for Edgar and went over to the clubhouse to swim. Punkin Head was already there. So was my friend Lily. "This is my foster grandpa," she said. "His name is Al."

We all shook Al's hand. "He used to work on the railroad," said Lily proudly.

"And he might take me for a ride to Chicago on Amtrak."

Al had a mustache and gray hair. You could tell he was from the city because his skin was so white. He wasn't sunburned like we all were. He dived into the pool at the deep end.

"Come on over this afternoon," Lily said to me. She bumped into me accidentally on purpose.

"I can't," I said.

"You can ride my new ten-speed," she said.

That's just like her to try and bribe me. Before I could answer, Marcy and Daisy brought George around to meet us. They were giving him a tour of Huckleberry Heights. He was real tall and skinny. I wouldn't call him cute. Cute is what Smiley is, all round and furry and bouncy. He reminded me of Eddie Haskell on *Leave It to Beaver*. The kind of kid who says polite things to impress grown-ups.

"We raise Siamese kittens," he said.

43

Big deal, I wanted to say. But instead I said, "We've got a sheepdog." Just in case he got any ideas of selling Marcy a kitten.

Punkin Head popped up out of the pool with his hair dripping down over his eyes. His trunks were too small for him, like most of his clothes.

"I'm saving my appetite for tonight," he said. "I'm not eating all day because Hilary is such a good cook."

After the swim we squished home in the wet street. It was still raining. I didn't see that sun Hilary talked about.

About five o'clock Hilary was mixing up her barbecue sauce in the kitchen. Smiley was sitting by the counter watching her.

"Do you want some barbecue too?" she said to him. "Good dog, Smiley." Smiley's tail wagged.

"I think I'll make a grill for Smiley too," she said. She put the steak to marinate in the barbecue sauce, and got wieners out for Smiley. She cut them up in little pieces with some leftover carrots and peas. She added some cheese and hardboiled eggs and rice and put a little barbecue sauce over the whole thing.

"That looks good," I said. "I wouldn't mind eating it myself."

"It's good nutritious food," said Hilary. "Not as good as steak, but tasty. Smiley will have a good treat."

She put it into a big pan on the counter. "We'll heat it up on the grill along with our steaks. We'll give the doggy a change from that old dry dog food, won't we, old fellow?"

Hilary leaned down and gave Smiley a kiss on his shaggy head.

Edgar and Lenny and Punkin Head came to the back door just then and flew in to get out of the rain. They were all dressed up in clean shirts and their hair was combed back as if they were going to church or something.

46

Then Marcy and Daisy and the Nelsons came in and we started this game of Parcheesi and it felt like a party. The Nelsons had cat hair all over them. Smiley kept hanging around George and sniffing him. "Maybe I can help in the kitchen instead of playing a game," said George.

Hilary was impressed, but she said no thanks.

My mom burst in the front door with a big bakery box and a black umbrella.

"It's really coming down!" she cried.

"I guess we'll have to cook inside," said Hilary.

"We have too many people for inside," I whispered to Marcy. It was getting crowded, and both doorbells began to ring at once.

I let Lily in at the back, and she wasn't even invited.

At the front door Hilary was saying, "Why, what a surprise!" Smiley barked. And my mom and Marcy were passing hors d'oeuvres around on little plastic plates.

"What a fine party," said Mrs. Nelson.

Hilary was talking to some man at the front door. "This is my cousin from Vermont, everyone. The one who makes maple syrup. He is just passing through on the way to Wisconsin."

Everyone shook the cousin's hand. My mom invited him to stay for the barbecue. Hilary went to the kitchen to put the meat in the broiler.

"Oh, no!" she cried. "Where is our barbecued steak?"

"Where did you leave it?" asked my mother.

"Right here on the counter," said Hilary. "Right here beside Smiley's dinner."

Sure enough, there was Smiley's dinner just where Hilary had left it. But the meat that was beside it was gone.

Marcy and Gus and my mom and I searched everywhere. In the refrigerator. In the oven. Even in the bedrooms.

"Where could it be?" said Hilary.

"It has no legs, it couldn't get up and walk away," said my mom.

Back in the kitchen, I noticed little red dots of barbecue sauce trickling across the counter and down on the floor.

"Somebody stole it," I said. "Look." I felt like a detective.

My mom looked closely. "Sure enough, Anthony is right. But who would steal our steak?"

I thought of Punkin Head right off. But even he wouldn't eat raw meat.

A clap of thunder sounded, and up from the basement came Smiley. He had an embarrassed grin on his face. And he looked different somehow. He burped.

"What's that red stuff on Smiley's face?" said Hilary. "I hope it isn't blood."

Gus knelt down and grabbed Smiley's face. "It's barbecue sauce," he said. "I can smell it!"

"He ate our dinner," cried my mother.

"It's my fault," said Hilary. "I left the meat, to answer the front door."

My mom put her arm around Hilary. "It's not your fault, Hilary. You didn't know that Smiley could reach the top of the counter. He is a tall dog when he stands on his hind legs."

"Bad dog!" I said. "Bad Smiley."

"He's not a bad dog," said Marcy. "He was hungry and Gus forgot to feed him."

Gus was busy playing Old Maid with all his guests.

"The question is, what will we serve them?" said my mother, going through the refrigerator. She took out the salad and some olives and pickles.

Everything else was frozen hard.

"You said Smiley's food was nutritious," I said.

"That's what we'll do," said Hilary. "We'll serve it with some crackers and cheese."

"Oh, we couldn't!" said my mom.

"We have to," I said, putting the tray in the oven.

My mom explained what happened to our steaks. And that the grocery stores had closed at six.

What she didn't explain was that because Smiley had eaten our dinner, we were eating his.

"This stuff is good," said Edgar.

"I'll bet it's loaded with vitamins," said Lenny.

Punkin Head was the only one who complained. "We were supposed to have steaks," he said. "I saved my appetite for steaks."

But no one went away hungry. If they didn't have enough of the dog food, they ate salad, and the cream puffs for dessert.

"What a shame Smiley had to ruin

your dinner," said George to my mom. "But all's well that ends well."

I wanted to point out that our dinner wasn't ruined, and if he hadn't mentioned it everyone would have forgotten. I didn't see what Marcy and Daisy saw in this overgrown kid.

That night Hilary told us more stories of growing up on the farm in Kansas. She told us how her brother took up magic and gave shows in their barn.

"He could pull a rabbit right out of my sleeve," she said.

"I thought rabbits got pulled out of hats," said Gus.

"That was how talented my brother was," said Hilary. "He pulled a gold watch out of a hat. And rabbits out of sleeves."

I fell asleep and dreamed about barbecued steaks being pulled from hats, and Smiley chasing a big white rabbit on a farm in Kansas.

The next week my mom took some time

53

off from work, and she and Hilary and Marcy and Daisy went to a lot of garage sales. Hilary bought some old tools. "I like to work with wood," she said.

For a few days she hammered away in our basement, and when she came up she had an eye-shadow rack for Marcy's little bottles and cases. She made one for Daisy, too, only it held her fingernail polish.

After that she said Smiley's doghouse could use a little porch so he could get air but not the hot sun. She worked on that for three days. Smiley loved it. He lay on a little rug my mom gave him and watched squirrels.

One morning my mom came downstairs and said, "You know, I think we should have a garage sale too. There's a lot of old stuff we don't need anymore."

Daisy and Marcy were reading *Vogue* at the kitchen table. "My mom wants to have one next Saturday," said Daisy. "Maybe we should combine them."

"You just tell me what you want to sell," said Hilary, "and I will price it and put it on tables."

Hilary loved to work. Sometimes it felt like we had a maid instead of a foster grandma.

I went through my room and found a basketball I never played with, and Gus had an old rocking horse he had outgrown. I brought a big box of stuff downstairs.

"All the curtains from our apartment that don't fit this house can go," said my mom.

Marcy and Daisy got busy scouring their rooms.

"Hey, who'd want that old tennis racket?" I said to Marcy. "It's all unstrung."

"It can be repaired," said Hilary.

I noticed Hilary always defended whichever one of us needed it.

When Edgar and Lenny heard about the sale, Edgar said, "Can I bring my

old set of encyclopedias over? They are out of date but everything in them is still eccentric."

When Edgar spoke like this, I had to think for a while. I knew Edgar was eccentric, but I didn't think his books were.

"Do you mean authentic?" asked Lenny.

"Yeah, authentric."

"Can Edgar bring his authentric encyclopedias over?" I asked my mom.

"Fine," she said. "I'll tell you what we'll do. We'll take the car out of the garage, and anything else we don't want to sell. Then we'll put everything for the sale, and the Otises' sale, in our garage and driveway. Then Hilary can label it."

"I'll get right to work," said Hilary.

All week we loaded the garage with stuff. Old clothes and a toaster without a cord and the rocking horse and even some things my mom had bought at other garage sales and was through with.

Hilary put an ad in the paper for the following Saturday. All week she put prices on things. It looked just like a department store when she was through.

"I'm going to buy a magic set with the money I get from my rocking horse," said Gus.

We sat on the back steps and added up in our heads how much we should get altogether.

"My books are worth a lot," said Edgar. "I might get ten dollars."

It was fun to think about getting rich from selling all our stuff. Maybe I'd think about being a salesman instead of a commercial fisherman.

"Hey, we could go through people's garbage and find lots of good things," said Lenny.

"We could be real exercising!" said Edgar.

I started hooting with laughter. But

58

Hilary was outside hanging clothes on the line and overheard him.

"He means enterprising," she said. "It's easy to mix those two words up."

I didn't think it was.

"Let's get our bikes and go look for good stuff," said Lenny.

We rode and rode around Huckleberry Heights looking in people's trash cans. It was Friday, the day the truck picked up.

"Hey, there's a good chair," said Lenny. "It looks brand-new."

"We can't carry a chair," said Edgar. "No way."

Everything we saw that was good was too big. Then we saw this little wood saw. "I could sell this to Hilary," said Lenny. "She likes tools."

"I'm going to buy a ten-speed bike too," said Gus on the way home.

Gus and I had old bikes compared with Edgar's and Lenny's. That's because my mom believed in kids working for stuff they wanted. And so far Gus and I had not worked hard enough, so we had these old one-speeds but they got us around.

By the time we got home, it was starting to rain.

"I hope," Hilary was saying, "that we don't have another barbecue experience."

"An indoor garage sale, you mean," said Marcy.

Hilary worked late into the night with last-minute items. I could hear her moving stuff around in the garage even after I was in bed.

The next morning was bright and sunny for the sale. It was a Saturday, so Mom was home. The Otises came to work, and Hilary and my mom and my aunt Fluffy had aprons on and pencils behind their ears.

Edgar and Lenny and Gus and I hung around for a while to see if our stuff was moving. Then Punkin Head came by and said, "Psst. Let's go down to

Uncle Sam Street. The guys left the tractors in the middle of the street."

Sometimes the workmen left their machinery on weekends and we pretended we were bulldozing big piles of dirt. We got up in the driver's seat and made noises like the bulldozer was running. During the week the workmen yelled at us when we got in their way, but on Saturday it was clear sailing.

"We'll be right back," I called to my mom. I don't think she heard me because she was trying to talk a lady into buying the rocking horse. The guys left their bikes in the backyard and we walked down to Uncle Sam Street.

Some of the bulldozers were so high, we had to stand on each other's shoulders to get to the cab.

"Look at me!" shrieked Gus.

It felt like we were on top of the world in those things. The wind blew through our hair and the sun beat down on us. I pretended I was one of the workers with

great big muscles and all this power. I could smash anything with this machine! *Zoom.* Out of my way. If I could start this thing, I could dig a new street or a basement for a house, just like that.

Maybe I'd be a construction worker when I grew up. I'd be all sunburned and have a line on my face where my hard hat came. I'd move mountains and earn a lot of money.

We all sat in our own machine. I wished I had a camera and could take our pictures.

It was so much fun digging roads and holes and driving those things that a couple hours went by before we remembered the sale.

"Let's go back and see how much money we earned," said Lenny.

By the time we got back, almost all the stuff was gone. The garage was almost empty. Marcy and Daisy were sweeping the driveway, and there were only some old clothes left that nobody wanted.

Hilary handed us envelopes with our names on them. It felt like I was getting a paycheck.

"Yikes!" said Lenny, tearing his open. "I got nine dollars!"

"I got ten dollars for my books!" shouted Edgar.

But I got the most, and I didn't think I'd had that much to sell.

"Fifteen dollars?" I said.

"It was a great sale," said Mrs. Otis. "A good turnout because of the hot, sunny day."

"We should do this more often," said my mom. "Things pile up that a person doesn't use."

We all stretched out on the front lawn. Then Gus said, "Let's go to the mall and spend our money."

Everyone got up and hopped on their bikes. Except me. "Where is my bike?" I asked, looking around.

The yard was empty. The garage was empty.

"Where did you leave it?" asked my mom.

I had to think. When we came home last night, it was raining.

"In the garage," I said.

Hilary clapped her hand over her mouth. "Oh, no!" she said with a gasp. "I'm afraid I sold your bike, Anthony!"

My bike was gone. Hilary sold my bike. That explained how I had more money than I should from the sale.

"How much did you get for it?" asked Lenny the businessman.

"A nice lady offered me ten dollars for it and I took it," said Hilary.

"You could have got more than ten dollars for that bike," whispered Punkin Head in my ear.

"I didn't want to sell it. I wanted to ride it," I said.

"It's my fault," said Hilary. "I'll buy you a new bike, Anthony."

"No, no," said my mother. "We did say that everything in the garage was for the sale. Anthony shouldn't have put it in the garage."

My mom was right. It wasn't Hilary's fault. I couldn't let her buy me a new bike, although the thought was tempting. I'd just put my bike in the garage out of habit. Because it was raining. But why would she sell a perfectly good bike for ten dollars?

I didn't feel like going to the mall now. I sure didn't feel like spending the bike money. It felt like blood money. Those wheels were my freedom.

"Tough luck," said Edgar, patting me on the back.

"You can buy a new one," said Lenny.

"That was rotten of her to sell your bike," said Punkin Head. "I know a place that has good deals on bikes. This old gas station down in St. Paul, you have to ask for a guy named Charlie . . ."

I didn't want any of Punkin Head's shady deals. I didn't want a pat on the back. I didn't even want another bike. What I wanted was my old rusty one back.

That night my mom came to my room and said, "We'll get you another bike, Anthony. I'll pay for half of it, if you can earn the other half. This is a good chance for you to get a better bike."

"Really?" I said. That sounded like a real good deal until I remembered I had no job and it wouldn't be easy earning money. Bikes were expensive.

"We'll figure out a way," said my mom, giving me a good-night kiss.

All night I tossed and turned trying to think of a way to earn money. Most jobs you had to be older.

At breakfast, Hilary whispered, "Let me chip in, Anthony. I'd like to help."

"I can handle it," I lied.

When Edgar came by, I rode on his handlebars and we went down to the creek. The creek runs behind the church on Silver Bell Lane. It's a nice secret place to sit and think. Or talk. The other guys were already there. We poked sticks in the water.

"I need a job," I said.

"You could be an errand boy," said Edgar. "The guy at the drugstore in the mall has a sign up, 'Delivery boy wanted.'"

"I need a bike to do that," I said. "I couldn't walk all over, it would take me forever."

"How about walking pets?" asked Lenny. "I'll bet Mrs. Hood would like you to walk Rex."

"And you could walk Elliot," offered Edgar. "All he does is sleep all day in the sun, the fat cat. He could use some exercise."

"I could do that, I suppose," I agreed. I was good with animals. There must be lots of pets in Huckleberry Heights that wanted to get out and have a social life. I could even brush them and teach them tricks.

Lily had joined us. She was sailing little sticks in the creek as if they were boats.

"My cousin," she said, "washes people's cars. And he cuts grass and stuff."

The people in Huckleberry Heights didn't cut their own grass. The condo association got people to do that. But I could certainly wash cars. Good old Lily. When she wasn't on my case, she could be useful.

Punkin Head came up with lots of ideas, but they all seemed just a little borderline. "Talk to your old lady," he whispered in my ear like it was a big secret. "Get her to give you a bigger allowance. Tell her you can't get along without a bike. Get down on your hands and knees, man, beg."

"I want to earn it," I said.

Punkin Head sighed. "You're hopeless," he said.

I waved to the kids and started for the clubhouse. I decided to put up a sign on the bulletin board there. Everybody would see it. There were lots of signs up already, like SKATES FOR SALE. Who would want ice skates in summer?

And BABY-SITTING IN MY HOME. That gave me an idea. I could baby-sit. Kids liked me. And I was reliable. I took a tack out of the board and put my sign up. It said, PET TENDING, CAR WASHING, BABY-SITTING. CALL TONY. Then I put my phone number.

I went for a swim with Marcy and Daisy and old George, and then went home.

"You had a phone call," said Hilary when I came in. "Do you walk pets?"

"I walk pets and wash cars and baby-sit," I said. "I am going to earn enough to buy a bike."

"Why, Tony, what an industrious

71

boy! And what good training for the future."

I called back the number she handed me.

"I am Mrs. Olson," said the voice at the other end. "I am going out of town for the weekend and I would much rather leave Foxy with someone who would give him a walk, than in a kennel."

"Fine," I said.

"I'll pay you three dollars a day to keep him," she said.

We closed the deal, and I dashed over to Lilac Lane to collect Foxy.

Foxy was a mixed breed. But mostly Great Dane. He was twice the size I was.

"Here is his food," she said. "And feed him twice a day, no more."

When I got home, I tied Foxy to the back fence so I could break the news to my family. Inside, Marcy was holding a little Scottie dog.

"A man dropped him off," she said. "He

wants Spot to be walked and brushed, and if you could teach him to heel he'll pay you extra. What's going on, Tony?"

I told her. Then Hilary came in and said, "Mrs. Lens would like you to babysit the twins while she goes to the grocery store. She's going to drop them off in ten minutes." Hilary looked pleased with the good news. Mrs. Lens was a neighbor who lived a few blocks away on Tiger Tail Trail. I knew her twins. They were a year old. I remembered that Marcy sat for them once. I tried to remember if they still wore diapers.

They did. I needed help. "I'll pay you if you'll help me out," I said to Marcy.

"I would, Tony, but I've got my ballet lesson in half an hour."

Thank goodness Hilary was there. She bounced Jackie and Jody on her knees till I went out and broke up the dogfight between Foxy and Smiley. I had no idea that Smiley was so territorial.

73

I put water and dog food down for Foxy and Spot in the kitchen. The twins both began to cry when they saw the dogs.

"Wow wow!" they screamed, and hung on to my legs.

"I'll put the dogs in the basement for a minute," said Hilary.

I put Jackie on the floor and gave her my keys to play with. They were on a chain, and when I rattled them, Jackie laughed.

Jody felt damp, and while Hilary and I were putting a clean diaper on her Jackie disappeared.

"She can't even walk!" I shouted. "How did she get away?"

"She must creep on her hands and knees," said Hilary.

When we found her, she was eating dog food out of the dish on the kitchen floor. Hilary and I tried to scoop as much as we could out of her mouth, and she bit me. This sweet little kid had mean fangs.

"I think some went down," said Hilary. "But we got most of it."

"Don't they take a nap?" I asked Hilary.

"Mrs. Lens said they just got up," she replied. "They could use a nice walk. Mrs. Lens brought the double stroller along."

What luck. I could walk the babies and the dogs at the same time. They'd all get air, and I could teach Spot to heel as we walked along.

I was wrong. We were not even a block away when the twins were screaming "Wow wow!" and crying, and Foxy broke loose and dug up the Bensons' geraniums. When I got them all home, there was a note on the door from Hilary that she'd be right back, she'd taken an apple pie to a sick neighbor. And I couldn't get into the house because Jackie had lost my keys.

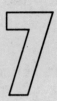

That night in bed I decided I didn't need a bike.

In the morning the phone woke me up at seven o'clock. It was a man who wanted his car washed before he left for work. I got up, found rags, washed the car, and took Foxy Olson for a walk. I was eating my breakfast at noon when Edgar came by with Elliot.

"Teach him to sit up," said Edgar. "He's bored because he can't do anything."

"I'll try," I said.

I did try. But it's hard to train cats and Elliot just flopped down like Jell-O when I sat him up. "He's a slow learner," I told Edgar.

That night Mrs. Olson took Foxy off my hands, and I added up all the money I'd earned so far. Six dollars for Foxy, three dollars for the twins, two dollars for Scottie, three dollars for the car wash, and a quarter from Edgar. Fourteen twenty-five. Not too bad, but new bikes were about two hundred dollars. It would take forever at this rate, and I didn't look forward to seeing Jackie and Jody again. I walked over to the clubhouse and took my sign down.

I was walking home wondering what to do, when Lenny came up on a bike, a different bike. He jumped off and kicked down the stand.

"What do you think?" he said, pointing to it.

The bike was a little rusty, but it had good tires and hand brakes.

"It's a three-speed," said Lenny. "It's for you."

"For me?"

"My dad picked it up at a sale where he works. He thought I might want it, but one bike is enough for me, and my dad said to give it to you when I told him about Hilary's mistake."

"Wow!" I said. I felt like hugging Lenny. What a good friend. I thanked him over and over, and then I went over to his house to thank his dad. Lenny and I rode down to the creek and past the new school and all around Huckleberry Heights. The new bike rode real smooth. And the chain didn't slip around like my old one did.

"I've got wheels again," I said. "I really missed my bike."

We went over to my house and I got out my car-washing rags and polished my new bike. I oiled the gears even though they didn't need it. Then I put it in the garage with a sign on it, DON'T SELL THIS BIKE.

My mom was home from work, and I couldn't wait to tell her my good luck. But before I could say anything, she called from the kitchen, "Anthony!" in a kind of musical way. My name *An-thon-y* had three notes. When she does that, she either wants me to do some job I won't like, or she has good news for me.

"Coming," I called. "I have something to tell you."

"I have something to tell you first," she said.

Marcy and Gus and Hilary were standing behind her with these big grins on their faces. Rosy-pink grins.

"Happy birthday, Tony!" they shouted.

"My birthday is six months away," I said.

"Well, happy birthday early, then," said Hilary.

I sat on the kitchen chair where my mom pointed.

She said, "Ta *da!*" and just then Aunt Fluffy came down the hall and into the kitchen wheeling this brand-new red ten-speed bike with a ribbon on it.

"For *me*?" I yelled.

"Hilary and I and Aunt Fluffy all chipped in," said my mom.

Gus look pouty.

"And Gus and Marcy each contributed —something," added Aunt Fluffy.

I couldn't believe this bike was for me. It was a racing bike with skinny tires. I rode down the hall while they all watched.

"You surely deserve a bike," said my mom. "After all the work you did to try to earn money."

"This way we won't have to—ah—entertain Jackie and Jody again," said Hilary. "Not that they aren't welcome . . ."

"I couldn't even manage those kids," said Marcy. "They never stopped moving."

81

I gave my entire family a hug, including my artificial grandma. "I'm really going to fly like the wind on this thing," I said. I didn't think it was the time to bring up Lenny's present. I'd keep it to myself for a while. Here I was, the owner of two bikes. I could ride one on rainy days and one on sunny ones. Or I could let some kid with no bike use the one Lenny gave me.

I called Edgar on the phone to tell him. I even called Lily, I was so happy. Then Marcy and I carried the bike outside and took off the bow. We rode and rode, all over Huckleberry Heights. Smiley ran along behind us, his ears blowing and flapping in the wind.

When we got home, I waited till Marcy went in the house. Then I opened the garage and parked my new shiny bike right next to my new rusty bike. I gave them both a pat, and shut the door.

All night I dreamed I was riding. Up and down hills and over bridges. I dreamed I rode all the way in to St. Paul to our old apartment. On the way back to Huckleberry Heights I went down a great big steep hill and my brakes didn't work. Just when I was about to crash, I woke up.

Someone was knocking on my window. "Psst," said a voice. "Hey, Tony. Get out here."

I'd know Punkin Head's voice anywhere.

"I'm asleep," I said through the screen.

"I gotta see you," he said.

I got my jeans on and went out in the backyard.

"Look what I got for you," he said proudly. "I got it at the dump."

Punkin Head was sitting on a very old bike. It had no fenders, and a lot of the spokes were broken. One tire was flat and the seat was missing.

"Look at this, the light really works," he said, flicking it on and off. "You can even ride at night."

I sat down on the back steps.

"Just these parts alone are worth money," he said, tapping on the back reflector. It had a crack across it. "I saw it in the dump and I said, hey, here is the answer to ol' Tony's problems."

"Great," I said to Punkin Head. "That's great of you to think of me."

He urged me onto this thing, and before I got out of the backyard, the gears fell off.

"I can fix that," said Punkin Head.

Yesterday I was a kid with no wheels. Today I had six of them. After Punkin Head connected the chain, I put it in the garage next to the other two. Punkin Head was already down the street telling Lily about the gift he gave me. I was afraid to go to the door for the rest of the day wondering who would show up next with a bike for me.

"What good friends you have, Anthony!" said my mom that night. "Good friends and hard work pay off."

"You don't need three bikes," said Gus.

"I'll keep them just in case," I said.

"Just in case there is another garage-sale mistake," said Hilary.

One evening when Hilary went to bed early, my mom and I played a game of Scrabble together. She liked words like *parabola* and *chalice*. Words that were musical. She'd lose points just turning in her letters every turn till she got ones that spelled a musical word. I used up letters with words like *dirt* and *it* and *cat*, but not my mom. "A good word or no word" was her philosophy.

I put down *lonely* to use up my *l*'s,

and my mom said, "I think Hilary is lonely."

"I don't," I said as she used my *y* to make *osprey*. "She is busy every minute."

"Busy, yes," said my mom. "But she has not been away from us since she arrived, Anthony. I think she could use a friend her own age—to go walking with or maybe fishing."

I put down *carp*.

"Day in, day out," my mom droned on, "she mostly sees children."

I shrugged my shoulders.

My mom made *pianola* with my *p* from *carp*.

Personally, I thought we were enough for Hilary.

"Keep your eyes open, Anthony, see if you can find a friend for Hilary."

All the letters were gone, and my mom won because she used all her letters in *finesse* and got fifty extra points.

"I don't think that's a real word," I said. She handed me the dictionary.

"Did you hear me, Anthony? See if you can find a friend for Hilary."

"I'll try," I said.

In the morning when the guys came over, we sat on the front steps. Hilary was giving Smiley a bath in the backyard.

"Hilary needs a friend," I said. "One her own age."

Lenny loved a problem to solve. I could see his mind spinning with ideas.

"Does she go to the grocery store?" he said. "There are lots of people her age in the grocery store in the mall."

I shook my head. "My mom gets the groceries," I said. "She has the car."

"How about the clubhouse?" asked Edgar. "Does she swim?"

"I don't think so," I said.

"What she needs is to join a club," said Marcy. "A club is the place to meet people."

"There's a club at the mall for sky divers!" said Punkin Head, jumping up from the steps.

"Hilary can't skydive," I scoffed. Punkin Head sat down again.

We thought and thought. The sun was hot on our heads. There must be someone who could be Hilary's friend.

"Hi," said a voice from around the back of the house. Lily was coming from her aunt's house next door. She plopped herself down in the tiny space between Marcy and me. She smelled like toothpaste.

"What are you doing?" she asked me.

"Thinking," I said. "Of a friend for Hilary. Somebody her age."

"Psst!" whispered Punkin Head. He motioned me down to the driveway. Then he whispered in my ear, loud enough for the whole neighborhood to hear. "I've got the answer."

"What?" I said.

"You got a grandma here," he said. "And Lily's got a grandpa. Put two and two together." He winked at me.

"We should get my grandpa and your

grandma together!" said Lily all of a sudden.

"That's what I said," said Punkin Head.

"I think they should date," said Lily dreamily.

I had to admit it felt right. Lily's grandpa Al must be lonely too.

"We'll fix them up," Lily went on. "Then they'll fall in love. Isn't that romantic?"

"Hilary just needs a friend, not a husband," I said, nipping Lily's matchmaking urges in the bud.

"It would be romantic," said Daisy, who had joined us now. "They could go for long walks."

"And picnics," said Marcy.

"And movies," said Edgar.

"They could even join the skydiving club," said Punkin Head.

"Where can they go on their first date?" said Lily. "Somewhere with moonlight, where they can hold hands."

Girls saw romance everywhere. Lily could take a good idea and turn it into hearts and flowers and wedding bells before they even met.

"We need a plan," said Lenny. "To get them together."

Edgar took a pencil and paper out of his pocket.

We all thought real hard.

"Could they meet accidentally on a walk?" I asked.

Edgar wrote down *Plan A: A walk.*

"Hilary doesn't go on walks," said Gus.

Edgar erased plan A.

"We could get her to take one," said Marcy.

Edgar wrote *Plan A* again.

"She'd be suspicious," said Gus.

"I'm getting a hole in the paper," said Edgar. "Let's put down a plan B in case we need it."

"A blind date," said Lily.

I got this funny picture in my mind of a stuffed date with powdered sugar on it, with no eyes. *Help,* it called out. *I can't find me a cookie to live in.*

"That's when friends fix them up but they don't know ahead of time who they are going out with," Lily went on.

Edgar wrote down *Plan B: Blind date.*

"We should have three plans," said Lenny. "My dad said always have options."

"What about a letter," said Daisy. "A kind of love letter."

Edgar wrote *Plan C: A mysterious letter.*

"Let's try the walk first," said Lily.

We set it up for one o'clock.

After lunch, Marcy said, "It's a nice afternoon out. I think we should take a walk. Get some exercise." Marcy stretched.

My mother was home for lunch. "I'd like that," she said. "Let's go."

Marcy hadn't thought of this complication.

"You have to go back to work, Mom," I said.

"I have plenty of time for a walk,"

94

she said. "I like to see what's new in the neighborhood."

"Nothing is," said Marcy. "Not a thing."

I looked at the clock. It was one minute to one. Lily and her grandpa would be coming by in one minute. Sure enough, I could see them now through the big front window. Al was stopping to pull some crabgrass and dandelions on the edge of our lawn.

Hilary was putting the lunch dishes in the sink. Gus ran outside, and I could see him talking to Lily. Lily stamped her foot and looked impatient. When he came in, he whispered, "Lily can't keep him out there much longer."

"Leave those dishes, Hilary," I said. "Go for a walk with Marcy."

I gave her a little shove in the direction of the door.

"I was going to watch my soap opera," said Hilary.

"Bad for your eyes, too much TV," I said.

95

Hilary laughed. "I suppose you're right," she said. "You seem to want me out of the house today."

My mom looked rejected, but she didn't say any more. After all, we were doing this for her. It was her idea Hilary needed a friend.

When they got outside, Marcy said, "Why, Lily, imagine meeting you out here taking a walk too! You know my foster grandma, Hilary, don't you?"

"Hello," said Lily. "This is my foster grandpa, Al."

I watched from behind a car so I could see them shake hands. But they didn't. They just said hello politely, and walked in opposite directions.

"It's not working," said Punkin Head, who had come by with Edgar to watch.

But Marcy quickly swung Hilary around and marched her back to Al and Lily.

"Maybe we could take a walk together," said Marcy.

"What a good idea," said Lily, walk-

ing behind with Marcy so that Al and Hilary could be together.

"They aren't saying anything," said Punkin Head. "Why aren't they talking?"

"Give it time," said Edgar. "Rome wasn't built in a day."

They walked all the way around the block, and I didn't see them say a thing except we needed rain. When they came to Lily's house, Al waved and turned in the yard.

"Isn't he a nice man!" said Marcy enthusiastically. "Lily said he is very lonely."

"Maybe he needs a hobby," said Hilary kindly. "A person isn't lonely when he keeps busy. I think I can catch the end of my show if I hurry."

Hilary dashed in the house and Edgar said, "So much for plan A."

Plan B was a blind date. I asked Hilary that night if she'd like to have one.

"Oh, no, Anthony," she said, looking puzzled. "I have wonderful friends right in this family." She gave me a hug, and walked to the kitchen to fill Smiley's water dish and give him some leftovers from supper.

"Plan C will not fail," I said the next day.

"Al will write a letter to Hilary," said Lily. "A love letter."

We decided Lenny should write the letter. I got a clean piece of notebook paper.

Dear Hilary, he wrote. *I have been admiring you from afar. I would like to be your friend and do stuff together. Love, Al. P.S. Maybe we could get married sometime.*

"I think it's too soon get married," I said.

"Al and Hilary are senior citizens," said Lily. "It's definitely not too soon to marry."

Lily knows more about that mushy stuff than I do, so I didn't argue. I took the letter and put it through our mail slot.

"Now," said Marcy. "All we have to do is wait. Tomorrow at this time Hilary should have a new friend her own age."

Tomorrow didn't work out quite the way I'd planned. In the morning Hilary announced at breakfast, "Someone sent me a forged note."

Marcy and Gus and I almost choked on our oatmeal. I didn't like the word *forged*. It had an illegal feeling about it. It was one thing to be laughed at for sending a phony letter. It was another thing to end up in jail.

Hilary passed the note around the table. I hoped Gus wouldn't blurt out, "I already read this." He didn't. He just said, "What is forged?"

"It's signing someone else's name and pretending it is yours," said my mother. "It's a crime."

At the word *crime,* Gus yelled, "I didn't do it."

"Of course you didn't," said Hilary kindly.

Marcy studied the note as if she'd never seen it before.

"How do you know it's forged?" she said with a brightness she couldn't have felt.

"Because it is a child's handwriting," said my mom. "And it's on school notebook paper."

"And why would Al write to me?" asked Hilary.

"It has no stamp on it," said my mother, studying the envelope. "Only U.S. Post Office mail is legally to be put in a mailbox."

Oh, boy. I wondered how come Lenny

didn't know about forgery. I always thought he was so smart.

"It's a puzzling thing," said Hilary, shaking her head. She cleared the oatmeal dishes away and Marcy helped her. "Maybe I should give Al a call."

I felt good about that for a minute. That's what we wanted—Hilary to call Al. Then I remembered he would deny writing the note. Why didn't we think of that before? I decided the best thing was to come clean. I followed my mom to her room after breakfast and said, "Lenny wrote that note."

"Why ever would he do a thing like that?" said my mother in surprise.

"You asked me to get a friend for Hilary, and the other ways didn't work. So we thought a letter might."

"What other ways?"

"A walk and a blind date."

"Why didn't you just introduce them if you thought they would like to meet?" said my mother sensibly.

103

"We never thought of that," I said.

Of course. That would have been the simple way. The easy way. The truthful way. The direct way.

"It was good of you to try," said my mother. "That was a very generous thing to do."

"Then Lenny won't go to jail?" I asked.

"Of course not," said my mother. "I think we should just ask Al over for dinner to get to know Hilary, and see if they'd like each other for friends. That seems the sensible thing to do."

"Good," I said.

That afternoon I explained things to Edgar and Lenny and Punkin Head and told them about forgery.

"I thought a forgery was where guys made horseshoes," said Edgar. We were ready to laugh at Edgar's mixed-up words until I looked it up in the dictionary, and sure enough, he was right. I looked at him with new respect. "That's the other kind of forge," I said.

"And there's Valley Forge," said Edgar, not wanting to stop a good thing. "And when you forge ahead to get something."

"Well, I'm not signing anybody's name again," said Lenny. "But my own."

The next Saturday we decided to go over to the clubhouse to see what was going on.

When we got in, there was a big sign on the bulletin board.

JOIN, JOIN, JOIN! it said.

" 'Try out for the Huckleberry Heights Baseball Team,' " read Lenny. " 'Open to all children under fourteen years of age.' "

"Oh, boy!" said Punkin Head. "I want to join."

"So do I!" said Edgar.

I always dreamed of being a pitcher. In a flash I could see myself dusting off the mound, spitting on the ground, and taking a good look around to see if anyone was sneaking off first base. The crowds would cheer in the stands and call out, "Tony! Tony! He's our man!" In that minute in the clubhouse I could feel the wind in my hair, the rain on my face, the ball in my glove. I could smell the peanuts and hot dogs, and see the flashing scoreboard.

"Where do we go?" I said. "When do we start?"

"There's a telephone number," said Edgar, squinting at the small print through his thick glasses.

"Hey," said Lenny. "It's your number, Tony!"

"Mine?" I repeated. "How could it be my number?"

I went up closer. It was my number.

"They made a mistake, they got one of the numbers wrong," said Gus.

But then we read the fine print. Underneath the number, it said, ASK FOR HILARY.

By the time we got to my house, there was a big bunch of kids in our living room. Hilary was writing down names in a notebook and my mom was passing out Kool-Aid. And you'll never guess who was passing out hats with CONDO KIDS on them. Al. Lily's artificial grandpa.

"Isn't this a great idea?" said my mom. "Huckleberry Heights with its own baseball team."

"Why didn't you tell us?" I asked Hilary.

"I wanted it to be a surprise!" said Hilary. "I stopped by the clubhouse last Tuesday and Al was there and said what a shame there was no baseball team. It's late in the season, but if we start now, you will be all organized for next spring!"

"We just got permission yesterday," said Al. "So we decided to move fast. It looks like we'll have enough for several teams!"

After all of our plans to get Hilary and Al together, they'd found each other all by themselves.

"Our plan worked," said Lily.

"They met on their own," I said. "At the clubhouse."

"Well, that was plan D," said Lily.

Al gave a little talk about team spirit and how everyone couldn't be a pitcher. "We'll meet Monday morning in the park," he said.

On Monday morning we found out Edgar couldn't pitch. His ball had a curve like a boomerang, and ended up almost back at his feet.

Everyone cheered when I pitched. I got chosen right off.

"Good for you, Tony," said Hilary.

We had enough players for two teams.

"The Condo Kids and the Hucksters," said Al.

All morning we practiced hitting balls. I was surprised how good a hitter Lily was. Marcy and Daisy needed lots of practice.

"This game is too hard on my fingernails," said Daisy.

"I hope she's not on my team," said Gus.

Hilary showed us how to bunt. And Al showed us how to hold the bat so we'd have the most power. He drew diagrams and little pictures of batters that said *right* and *wrong*.

"What is the matter with this picture?" he asked.

We all stared at the paper he held up.

"His hat is on backward," said Daisy.

"He's left-handed," said Punkin Head.

Al shook his head. "That doesn't matter," he said.

"He's facing the plate," said Lily.

"Exactly!" said Al. "A pitcher does not face the plate. Good for you, Lily."

That was my girl friend all right.

By the end of the week we were getting pretty good. We practiced every day in Liberty Park, and my mom and Aunt Fluffy and mothers with little kids came to watch. Even Smiley and Elliot watched.

The summer was going fast. My muscles started looking like the guy's muscles on the cover of *Wrestling*. Aunt Fluffy wrote a rouser for the fans to sing when we played a real game.

"Pretty soon Al and Hilary will be leaving," said Marcy one day. "And school will be starting."

I didn't want to think about that. I didn't want the summer with my artificial grandma to be over.

"Cheer up, Anthony," said my mom one evening when I looked kind of sad. "Tomorrow night is the dinner for Hilary."

"What dinner?" I said.

"The dinner to meet Al," she said.

We both laughed. "This can be her farewell dinner," said my mom.

And that's what it was. Everybody in Huckleberry Heights came, it seemed like. My mom put a chef's hat on and broiled steaks on the grill in the backyard. It didn't rain and Smiley didn't steal the meat. George and his family

111

were there again, and Lily and Al and the Otises and Pottses and Foxes and Punkin Head's family too.

We played lawn games and catch and threw the Frisbee for Smiley.

"This is a wonderful party," I overheard George say to my mom.

And then my mom tapped a spoon on a kettle and gave a little speech about how glad we were to have had Hilary with us. I could have cried.

"Hilary has brought joy to our life this summer," said my mom. "And I am sure we all learned a lot from her, and we treasure her as a new friend."

I wiped my eyes so no one would think I was a baby about this, and then Hilary stood up to talk. She thanked us for opening our home to her, giving her fresh air and new friends, and new experiences.

"You were supposed to meet Al at this party," Gus said. "And it was Lenny who wrote that note."

Everyone laughed, and Hilary said, "I was so surprised when I ran into Al at the clubhouse and found he liked baseball. I loved baseball even when I was Tony's age, and Al said that was what Huckleberry Heights needed—baseball for children. So we decided to get together and start a team. I'm sorry I ruined your plan to introduce us."

Everyone laughed some more and applauded.

"We don't want you to leave," said Edgar.

"Who's going to coach our team in spring?" said Lenny.

"I'll be back," said Hilary. "And I can keep in touch from St. Paul, you know."

The sun was going down and a cool breeze was coming up. I looked at all our friends in Huckleberry Heights and thought about what a nice place it was to live.

"Psst," said Punkin Head furtively, behind my back. "I've got a plan for Hilary and Al to stay . . ."

Lenny took out a notebook and pencil and wrote *Plan A.*

I knew the plan wouldn't work. Hilary and Al had to leave. But she would be our artificial grandma forever.

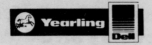

Nintendo 64
Power Pocket Guide:
Unauthorized

® is a registered trademark of
Prima Publishing, a division of
Prima Communications, Inc.

® and Prima Publishing ® are registered trademarks of
Prima Communications, Inc.

PRIMA

Project Editor: Brooke N. Raymond
Designed by: Prima Creative Services, England

All products and characters mentioned in this book are trademarks of their
respective companies.

Important:

ISBN: 7615-0971-2
Library of Congress Catalog Card Number: 96-070916
97 98 99 00 HH 10 9 8 7 6 5 4 3

ACKNOWLEDGMENTS

A million and one thanks must go to the boys who have put
such a lot of hard work into these game strategies and
designing the book on such a short deadline...

Paul Middleton
Simon Hill
Ian Osborne

Cheers lads!
Nick Roberts

CONTENTS

INTRODUCTION

I t's fast, it's furious, it's the greatest thing since…
well since the last Nintendo console!
The Nintendo 64 is with us, and looking mighty fine!
With its slick black appearance and cool joypads this
is a console that is ready to set the world on fire!

But what of the games that go along with it? In this
Pocket Power Guide we've taken every released
game and compiled top quality playing tips,
strategies, cheats, and codes for you to use to push
yourself up to the top of the high-score table.

We've got all the special beat-'em-up moves for
Mortal Kombat Trilogy and *Killer Instinct Gold*.
Complete racing tips for *Mario Kart 64* and *Cruis'n
USA*, sporting strategies for *Wayne Gretsky's 3D
Hockey* and *Wave Race 64*. We've even got the
complete low down on *Shadows of the Empire*, and
info on the classics *Super Mario 64* and *PilotWings 64*!

Phew! I think that's exhausted everything the
Nintendo 64 has to offer for now! Enjoy the book, and
watch out for more Nintendo 64 tips and strategies
very soon!

Nick Roberts

Nick Roberts

Cruis'n USA
Hidden Vehicles

On the car selection screen, hold the buttons C[U], C[D], and C[L] while cycling through the vehicles. From the left, the cars become a jeep, a school bus, and a police car. The car on the far-right doesn't change.

General Tips

● You always start from last place on the grid. Worry not—just pull to the left and accelerate. Chances are you're in the lead by the first bend.

● Remember, this is a road race. Driving on the right-hand side minimizes head-on collisions.

● Stay on the track. In terms of collision detection, the game is very generous when you leave the road, but driving on pavements and grass reduces your speed. The fastest way to drive is to keep on the track and drive as straight as possible.

● Watch out when climbing hills. You can't see through them, so take a glance at the radar to make sure you're not heading for a collision with a car you can't see coming the other way. Again, keep on the right too.

● Keep your speed up. Believe it or not, it's possible to be timed out while in the lead, so don't relax.

The Cars

When racing there's little to choose between the cars, but in theory they rank (best first) like so...

Acceleration		Speed	
1:	La Bomba	1:	Devastator VI
2:	Italia P69	1:	Police Car
3:	All Terrain Vehicle	3:	School Bus
4:	'63 Muscle Car	4:	Al Terrain Vehicle
5:	Police Car	4:	'63 Muscle Car
6:	Devastator VI	6:	Italia P69
7:	School Bus	7:	La Bomba

Road Holding

1:	School Bus
2:	Devastator VI
2:	Police Car
4:	'63 Muscle Car
4:	All Terrain Vehicle
6:	La Bomba
7:	Italia P69

The Courses

Golden Gate Park

Use the long, four-lane straightaway to get ahead. Speed across the Golden Gate Bridge, then to another long straightaway. There's another left just before the first checkpoint, and another immediately after it.

An easy right over a hill leads to the second bridge, followed by another right onto a marble bridge. Use this area to build speed, but watch out for oncoming cars. There's a checkpoint past the next hill—watch your radar. Don't worry about the barrels and posts on the straightaway—just plow through them. Another gentle curve takes you to yet another bridge. Two right/left drifts take you to a second marble bridge, which is as straight as an arrow but far from flat. An easy right takes you to the third checkpoint, a left takes you over another marble bridge, a second left takes you over yet another marble bridge, then get ready for a sharp left. You know it's coming when you see the Nintendo logo up ahead. Go flat out on the home stretch to the finish.

San Francisco

A sharp right crops up almost immediately, but by then you won't have built-up enough speed to make it tricky. The next section is a drive through the streets of San Francisco, with two-lane roads walled by buildings.

This makes life difficult, as collisions between other racers often cover the whole road, proving difficult to avoid. Make sure you stay ahead and on the track as you speed to the first checkpoint.

A right-hander leads to some very hilly territory, and the narrow streets make it difficult to stay right. Keep checking your radar, and hit the gas for a long straightaway, ending in a right. Release the accelerator for this one—it's not tricky, but by now you're really shifting. Another speedy but hilly straightaway ends in another right, leading to another straightaway through the second checkpoint. A long but gentle left leads to a sharp right/left, then into a tunnel.

The corners are all fairly gentle in the tunnel, but collisions are even trickier to avoid than in the outdoor stage. If a pile-up blocks the road, there's little you can do, but don't rub against the walls, and make sure you don't hit anything—you should keep up your speed. The finish line is inside the tunnel.

US 101

Starting at the end of the tunnel, go flat out past the right/left twist in the road, and you should be in the lead. Take the right fairly fast, but don't drift onto the gravel, or you lose speed.

What follows is a ridiculous jump over a chasm in the road—how do the ordinary drivers get over, I wonder? Stake it at speed, but don't worry if you fall into it—you reappear on the track with barely a pause. An easy left leads to the first checkpoint, which is followed by another easy left.

A couple more tight but fast turns and a second chasm leads to the second checkpoint, after more similar-sized turns taking you to the third. There's an incredibly tight right leading to the finish line—release the accelerator or you hit the gravel.

Redwood Forest

Narrow roads and tight bends make this a dangerous course. Thankfully, if you leave the road and hit a tree, you go through it as if it wasn't there. Do your utmost to get the lead by the time the road narrows into a hellish turn. A left leads to a short straightaway, followed by a right—signs indicate corners, so look out for them. Another right leads to a short straight section ending in a couple of lefts, and then the checkpoint.

The road swings right, left, then right again before entering a long, slow left. After this, it's more of the same leading to the next checkpoint. A few twists and turns later the forest gives way to desert and the road widens to four lanes. Go through the checkpoint and put the pedal to the metal—you're unlikely to be in the lead by now, so now is your chance to regain it. The bends are fairly simple on this section, and you should be able to gain several places.

Beverly Hills

Watch out for the roadside trees here—they aren't as forgiving as those in the Redwood Forest stage. The first turn is a sharp left— don't leave the road. A gentle right/left swerve leads to a short straightaway, ending in a short winding section. Then comes the first checkpoint. The next few turns are fairly nondescript, but look out for a sharp right as you approach Hollywood Hill.

The next section is full of gentle turns. Take the racing line, driving as straight as possible, and you can take it flat out.

There's an incredibly tight right after the next checkpoint though, so prepare for it in advance. You then enter a tunnel section which is, if anything, faster than the last. The turns are sharper, but touching the walls is less of a problem. Again the finish line is in the tunnel.

LA Freeway

Rocket out of the tunnel and take the first few bends flat out. Speed through the first checkpoint and keep your foot on the floor all the way to the second. Don't slow down on your way to the third, then power to the finish line. This is an easy course, with wide roads, gentle curves, and few Sunday drivers. There are no really tricky turns, and you should take the lead very quickly and keep it throughout the race.

Death Valley

Pick your way left and past the pack, taking the curve at the same time. Don't leave the road—you plow through the prickly plants, but lose an immense amount of speed. Pick up speed on the very long straightaway, but be careful—the track is extremely narrow, and one collision ahead of you can cost several places.

A long right leads to the first checkpoint. Follow the road signs left, then race down the straightaway. Careful when overtaking—you can't leave the road or you lose too much speed; if you overtake on the road, you risk a head-on smash. Run through the next checkpoint, then take the long right.

The next few turns, through the third checkpoint, are simple affairs, but the narrow track continues to make overtaking difficult. The road eventually widens as you approach the rail track. Don't hit the train as you cross the track. After this, it's a simple ride to the finish.

Arizona

After a short straightaway come two extremely tight right/left chicanes, followed by the first checkpoint. A couple of innocuous turns later there's a longer straight—build speed here. Then there are three sharp but simple rights and a straight to the second checkpoint. The next two turns, a left and a right, are trickier, but the long straight section interrupted by very mild turns makes up for this. After the third checkpoint the road twists and turns, but doesn't really test your driving skills. The run to the finish is a simple one.

Grand Canyon

This course is "more of the same," with winding roads and wide courses. Blind corners and hills cause problems—don't run into a driver coming the other way.

There's an incredibly sharp right after the first checkpoint. This is followed by more winding track, leading through the second and to the third. Don't worry about the telegraph poles on the way to the finish line—they fall if you hit them.

This course isn't too tricky. There are few challenging curves, but the hills and rocky mountains make it difficult to see what's coming next.

Iowa

The first bend, a left, causes no problems. The track soon narrows, though, and you're forced to blast your way through a toll plaza. Keep yourself straight as you batter through, then proceed to the next bend, a sharp banked right, a left, then another right to the checkpoint.

The next few turns are of similar ferocity, and are quickly followed by the next checkpoint. A couple of rights take you over the bridge, then after a few more winding turns, you hit another toll plaza. Try to go through one of the gaps, not the building itself.

Fly over the bridge to the last checkpoint. From there, it's a simple ride to the finish.

Chicago

Considering this is the "windy city," the smoke from chimney stacks rises surprisingly straight. Follow the road to the right, then build up speed before taking a sharp right. Put your foot down for the extreme straight, ending in a left and the checkpoint. Don't worry about hitting the flyover buttresses—you go right through.

Watch out for oncoming cars as you take the next bend, then get on the right-hand side of the road before entering the underpass. The posts in the center spin you around if you hit them, and driving on the wrong side here is a nightmare. The bends inside are taxing, but not drastic. Stick to the center area between the posts where the flyover is being built. After this comes the finish line.

Indiana

Despite the narrow track, this is an easy stage. The corners, though tight, are easy enough to get around and the telegraph poles along the roadside fall on contact.

An enormous straightaway sends you crashing through a toll plaza, then into a left turn. Hammer through the first checkpoint, then past a few reasonably tight turns to the second. Look out for a long, sharp left after this. Past the third checkpoint, there are a few turns, leading to the finish.

Appalachia

Here you start on a bend, but this presents no real problems. Little else does, either. If you watch out for corners and hills, you can blast through this stage.

Washington DC

The route to the first checkpoint has only gentle turns, making it almost as fast as a straightaway. It continues very much in this manner, except for a couple of hard rights near the Washington Monument and the White House. A very hard right soon follows, and another straight after the Vietnam War Memorial. This takes you to the next checkpoint. Make your way through the bridges and the tunnel to the finish.

KILLER INSTINCT GOLD
Play the Boss

You can play the game as Gargos by following these simple instructions: On the character story screen press **Z, A, Right Shoulder Button, Z, A, B**. If you've pressed the buttons correctly, you should hear a laugh and Gargos will appear on the character selection screen.

Secret Colors

Again on the character select screen press: **Z, B, A, Z, A, Left Shoulder Button.** You'll hear a sound effect play, if you pressed the buttons correctly, and the secret colors white, gold, and black will now be selectable in the same way as the normal colors.

Enable All Options

On the character profile screen press the following buttons: **Z, B, A, Left Shoulder Button, A, Z**. You'll hear the word "Perfect," if you pressed correctly, and all the options will be available.

View credits

To go straight to the credits without having to beat Gargos, go to the character profile screen and press the buttons: **Z, Left Shoulder, A, Z, A, Right Shoulder**. The credits will start to roll, if you did this correctly.

View High Scores

Just press **Z** during the demo. Press again to cycle through the various high score screens.

Random Character Select

On the character selection screen, press ↑ and **Start**. The computer selects your character at random.

Music and Stage Select

These codes only work in a two-player game. Instead of just pressing a button to select your character, use the codes offered here. Player One selects the scene, Player Two the tune. For example, to fight in Sabrewulf's lair with Orchid's tune, both players should highlight the character of their choice, then one should hold ↑ and press **QP**, the other holds **Up** and presses **FK**. To fight on the Sky Stage, both players must use ↓+**MK**.

Sabrewulf's Layer	↑ + QP
The Jungle (Maya)	↑ + MP
Glacius' Crash Site	↑ + FP
Stonehenge (Tusk)	↑ + QK
The Museum (Fulgore)	↑ + MK
The Helipad (Orchid)	↑ + FK
The Bridge (Jago)	↓ + QP
The Castle (Gargos)	↓ + MP
The Street (Combo)	↓ + FP
The Dojo (Kim-Wu)	↓ + QK
Skeleton Ship (Spinal)	↓ + MK
Sky Pad	↓ + MK (both players)

All Characters' Moves

FULGORE
Special Moves

Cyber Dash	↙, ↓, ↘ + MK or FK
Electro Flect	↓↙← + hold QK
Plasma Slice	→, ↓, ↘ + any Punch
Laser Storm	↓↘→ + any Punch
Fake Laser Storm	↓↙← + QP
Eye Laser	↘, ↓, ↙ + MP or FP
Spinning Slice	← + FK
Triple Laser Storm	←↙↓↘→ + QP

17

Super Moves

Super Electro Flect	↘, ↓, ↙, → + QK (3 Blocks)
Super Cyber Dash	↙, ↓, ↘, ← + FK (3 Blocks)
Lock On	←↙↓↘→ + QK (1 Block)
Plasmaport	←, ↓, ↙ +any Punch/Kick (1 Block)
Air Eye Laser	Jumping, ↘, ↓, ↙ + FP (1 Block)
Inviso	→↘↓↙← + FK (Any of the Blocks)

Finishing Attacks

Mini Ultra	→, ↓, ↘ + QP
Ultra Combo	→, ↓, ↘ + QK
Ultimate	→, ←↙↓↘→ + MK
O-Combo Ultimate	←↙↓↘→, ← + MP

Throws, Breakers and Counter-Moves

Combo Breaker	→, ↓, ↘ + any Punch or Kick
Ultra Breaker	↓, ↙, ←↙↓↘→ + FP
Air Double	→, ↓, ↘ + any Punch
Pressure Move	← + FP
Counter Dizzy	← + QP, Uppercut + QP
Parry Move	← + hold QP

GLACIUS

Special Moves

Cold Shoulder	↓↘→ + MP
Liquidize	↓↘→ + QK
Liquidize in Air	↓↘→ + any Kick
Liquidize/Uppercut	↓↘→ + MK or FK
Icy Grip	↓↘→ + QP
Arctic Blast	↓↙← + any Punch
Ice Lance	↓↘→ + FP
Energy Gain	↓↘→ + QK

Super Moves

Arctic Slam	↙, ↓, ↘, ← + QP (6 Blocks)
Super Arctic Blast	→↘↓↙←, → + FP (4 Blocks)
Super Cold Shoulder	↙, ↓, ↘, ← + MP (3 Blocks)
Super Liquidize and Uppercut	→↘↓↙← + FK (3 Blocks)
Super Uppercut	↙, ↓, ↘, ← + FK (3 Blocks)

Finishing Attacks

Mini Ultra	↓↙← + QK
Ultra	↓↘→ + QK
Ultimate	→↘↓↙←, → + MK
O-Combo Ultimate	↓, ←, ↙ + QK

Throws, Breakers and Counter-Moves

Throw	→ + FP
Throw Reversal	← + FP
Combo Breaker	↓↘→ + any Punch or Kick
Ultra Breaker	←↙↓↘→, ← + QP
Air Double	↓↘→ + any Kick
Pressure Move	→ + FK
Parry Move	← + hold QP

JAGO

Special Moves

Laser Blade	↘, ↓, ↙ + MP or FP
Windkick	↘, ↓, ↙ + any Kick
Ninja Slide	↙, ↓, ↘ + any Kick
Endokuken	↓↘→ + any Punch
Fake Endokuken	↓↘→ + QK
Red Endokuken	Hold FP, ←↙↓↘→ + release FP
Tiger Fury	→, ↓, ↘ + any Punch

Super Moves

Super Tiger Fury	↓, ↙, ←↙↓↘→ + FP (6 Blocks)
Super Endokuken	→↘↓↙← + QP (4 Blocks)
Super Ninja Slide	↙, ↓, ↘, ↓ + FK (3 Blocks)
Super Wind Kick	↘, ↓, ↙, → + MK (3 Blocks)
Shadow Move	↘, ↓, ↙, → + MK (3 Blocks)

Finishing Attacks

Mini Ultra	↙, ↓, ↘ + QK
Ultra	↘, ↓, ↙ + QK
Ultimate	→, ↓, ↘ + FK
O-Combo Ultimate	→↘↓↙←, → + MP

Throws, Breakers and Counter-Moves

Throw	→ + FP
Throw Reversal	← + FP
Combo Breaker	→, ↓, ↘ + any Punch or Kick
Ultra Breaker	↓, ↙, ←↙↓↘→ + FP
Air Double	↘, ↓, ↙ + any Kick
Pressure Move	→ + FK
Parry Move	← + Hold QP

KIM-WU

Special Moves

Tornado Kick	↘, ↓, ↙ + any Kick
Firecracker	↘, ↓, ↙ + MP or FP
Split Kick	↙, ↓, ↘ + FK
Fake Split Kick	↙, ↓, ↘ + MK
Fireflower	↓↘→ + QP
Air Fire	↓, ↘, → + MP or FP
Air Torpedo	Jumping, ↓, ↙, ← + any Punch
Roll	Tap →, →

Super Moves

Snap Dragon	↓, ↙, ←↙↓↘→ + FP (6 Blocks)
Super Air Tornado	Jumping, ↓↘→, ← + MP (4 Blocks)
Shadow Move	↘, ↓, ↙, ←→ + FK (3 Blocks)
Super Firecracker	↘, ↓, ↙, → + FP (6 Blocks)
Super Tornado	↘, ↓, ↙, ←→ + FK

Finishing Attacks

Mini Ultra	↘, ↓, ↙ + QK
Ultra	↙, ↓, ↘ + QK
Ultimate	←↙↓↘→, ← + QK
O-Combo Ultimate	←, →, ←↙↓↘→ + MK

Throws, Breakers and Combos

Throw	→ + FP
Throw Reversal	← + FP
Combo Breaker	→, ↓, ↘ + any Punch or Kick
Ultra Breaker	↓, ↙, ←↙↓↘→ + FP
Air Double	↓↘→ + any Punch
Pressure Move	→ + FK
Parry Move	← + hold QP

MAYA

Special Moves

Mantis	←, → + FP
Air Mantis	Jump, →, ← + FP
Savage Blades	←, → + MP
Flip Kick	←, → + MK
Jungle Leap	←, → + FK
Savage Leap	←, → + QK
Cobra Bite	←, → + QP

Super Moves

Super Jungle Leap	→↘↓↙←, → + FK (6 Blocks)
Super Flip Kick	→↘↓↙←, → + MK (3 Blocks)
Super Savage Blades	→↘↓↙←, → + MP (3 Blocks)
Shadow Move	→↘↓↙←, → + FP (3 Blocks)

Finishing Attacks

Mini Ultra	→, ← + FP
Ultra	→, ← + FK
Ultimate	→↘↓↙←, → + QK
O-Combo Ultimate	←↙↓↘→, ← + QP

Throws, Breakers and Counter-Moves

Throw	→ + FP
Throw Reversal	← + FP
Combo Breaker	←, → + any Punch or Kick
Ultra Breaker	→↘↓↙←, → + FK
Air Double	→, ← + any Kick
Pressure Move	→ + FK
Parry Move	← + hold QP

ORCHID

Special Moves

Flik Flak	↘, ↓, ↙ + any Kick
Ichi	↘, ↓, ↙ + MP
Tiger Slide	↙, ↓, ↘ + any Kick
Tonfa Fire	↓, ↘, → + any Punch
Fake Tonfa Fire	↓, ↘, → + QK
San	↘, ↓, ↙ + FP
Air Buster	→, ↓, ↘ + any Kick

Super Moves

Super Flak	↓, ↙, ←↙↓↘→ + FK (6 Blocks)
Super Ichi	↙, ↓, ↘, ← + FP (3 Blocks)
Fire Cat	↘, ↓, ↙, → + MK (3 Blocks)

Finishing Attacks

Mini Ultra	↙, ↓, ↘ + FP
Ultra	↘, ↓, ↙ + QK
Ultimate	→↘↓↙←, F + FP
O-Combo Ultimate	←, ↓, ↙ + MK

Throws, Breakers and Counter-Moves

Throw	→ + FP
Throw Reversal	← + FP
Combo Breaker	→, ↓, ↘ + any Punch or Kick
Ultra Breaker	↓, ↙, ←↙↓↘→ + FK
Air Double	↘, ↓, ↙ + any Kick
Pressure Move	→ + FK
Parry Move	← + hold QP

SABREWULF
Special Moves

Sabre Wheel	←, → + MP
Sabre Spin #1	←, → + MK
Sabre Spin #2	→, ← + MK
Sabre Pounce	←, → + FP
Sabre Flip	←, → + FK
Sabre Howl	←, → + QP
Fake Sabre Howl	←, → + QK
Sabre Hop	Tap →, → or ←, ←
Double Spin	→, →, ← + MP

Super Moves

Super Sabre Flip	→↘↓↙←, → + FK (6 Blocks)
Sabre Stomp	Jump, →↘↓↙← + FP (4 Blocks)
Sabre Fireball	→↘↓↙←, → + FP (4 Blocks)
Super Sabre Wheel	→↘↓↙←, → + MK (3 Blocks)
Super Sabre Spin	→↘↓↙←, → + MP (3 Blocks)

Finishing Attacks

Mini Ultra	→, ← + QK
Ultra	←, → + QK
Ultimate	Hold FK for two seconds, release
O-Combo Ultimate	Hold QP for two seconds, release

Throws, Breakers and Counter-Moves

Combo Breaker	←, → + any Punch or Kick
Ultra Breaker	→↘↓↙←, → + FK
Air Double	↘, ← + any Punch
Pressure Move	→ + FK
Parry Move	← + hold QP

SPINAL

Special Moves

Skele Skewer	↓↘→ + MP
Flame Blade	↓↘→ + FP
Skull Scrape	↓ + FK
Skull Spear	Jumping, ↓ + FK
Soul Drain	↓↘→ + QP
Skull Dash	Tap →, → or ←, ←
Skeleport	↓↙←, any Kick
Power Devour	← + hold QP
Searing Skull	↓↘→ + any Kick

Special Moves

All Skull Summon	↓↙← + FP (6 Blocks)
Super Searing Skull	↓, ↙, ←↙↓→ + FK (6 Blocks)
Stunning Skull	↓, ↙, ←↙↓→ + MK (4 Blocks)
Super Grim Reaper	↓, ↙, ←↙↓→ + FP (4 Blocks)
Super Skull Screpe	↓↘→, ← + FK (3 Blocks)
Super Flame Blade	↓↘→, ← + MP (3 Blocks)
One Skull Summon	↓↙← + MP (1 Block)

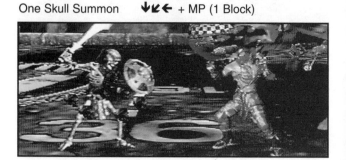

Finishing Attacks

Mini Ultra	↓↘→ + FP
Ultra	↓↙← + FP
Ultimate	↓, ↓ + QK
O-Combo Ultimate	↓↘→, ↓↘→ + QP

Throws, Breakers and Counter-Moves

Throw	→ + FK
Throw Reversal	← + FK
Combo Breaker	↓↙← + any Punch or Kick
Ultra Breaker	↓, ↙, ←↙↓↘→ + FK
Air Double	In the air, ↓ + any Kick
Pressure Move	→ + FP

T.J. COMBO

Special Moves

Air Tremor	Jump, ←↙↓↘→ + MK
T.J. Tremor	Charge ←, → + MK
Spinfist	Charge ←, → + QP
Spinfist/Hook	Charge →, ← + QP
Roller Coaster	Charge →, ← + MP
Double Roller Coaster	Charge ←, → + MP
Powerline	Charge ←, → + FP
Stop Powerline	← + FP
Skull Crusher	Charge ←, → + FK
Cyclone	Charge FP for 3 secs, release, FP
Fake Dizzy	→↘↓↙← + QK, any button to stop
Behind Back	Charge ←, → + QK
Backward Roll	←, ←

Super Moves

Dash Frenzy	→↘↓↙←, → + FP (2-6 Blocks)
Super Tremor	→↘↓↙← + MK (3 Blocks)
Super Roller Coaster	→↘↓↙←, → + MP (3 Blocks)
Super Spinfist	→↘↓↙←, → + QP (3 Blocks)
Shadow Move	→↘↓↙←, → + MP (3 Blocks)

Finishing Attacks

Mini Ultra	Charge ←, → + FK
Ultra	Charge →, ← + FP
Ultimate	Hold QK for 2 secs, release
O-Combo Ultimate	Charge →, →↘↓↙← + FK

Throws, Breakers and Counter-Moves

Throw	→ + MP
Throw Reversal	← + MP
Combo Breaker	←, → + any punch/kick
Ultra Breaker	→↘↓↙←, → + FP
Air Double	→, ← + any Kick
Pressure Move	→ + FK
Counter Dizzy	← + QP, Powerline + FP
Parry Move	← + hold QP

TUSK

Special Moves

Boot Kick	↘, ↓, ↙ + any Kick
Web Of Death	↘, ↓, ↙ + FP
Skull Splitter	↙, ↓, ↘ + FK
Fake Skull Splitter	↓↘→ + QK
Back Stab	→↘↓↙← + QP
The Conqueror	→, ↓, ↘ + any Punch
Spin High/Low attack	→ + FP

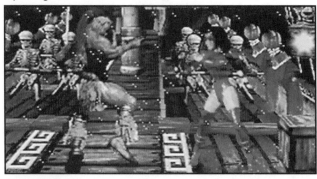

Super Moves

Super Conqueror	↓, ↙, ←↙↓↘→ + FP (6 Blocks)
Pillar of Flames	↙, ↓, ↘, ← + QK (4 Blocks)
Super Boot Kick	↘, ↓, ↙, → + FK (3 Blocks)
Super Web of Death	↓↘→, ← + FP (3 Blocks)
Shadow Move	↙, ↓, ↘, ← + FK (3 Blocks)

Finishing Attacks

Mini Ultra	←↙↓↘→ + MP
Ultra	→↘↓↙← + MP
Ultimate	→, ↓, ↘ + MK
O-Combo Ultimate	↓↘→, ↓↘→ + MP

Throws, Breakers and Counter-Moves

Throw	→ + FK
Throw Reversal	← + FK
Combo Breaker	→, ↓, ↘ + any Punch or Kick
Ultra Breaker	↓, ↙, ←↙↓↘→ + FP
Air Double	↘, ↓, ↙ + any Kick
Pressure Move	→ + FP
Parry Move	← + Hold QP

GARGOS

Enter the special code and you can play as the
Dark Lord Gargos!

Special Moves

Flame	↓↘→ + QP
Fly	↑ + FP (FK to land)
Jumping Overhead	
Slam Jump	↓↘→ + FP
Two-Handed Strike	←↙↓↘→ + FK
Air Fireball	Jump, ↓↘→ + FP
Shoulder Dash	→↘↓↙← + MK or FK
Laugh (reflects projectiles)	→↘↓↙← + FP
Uppercut	→, ↓, DF + FP

Throws, Breakers and Counter-Moves

Throw	→ + FP
Throw Reversal	→ + FK
Combo Breaker	↓↘→ + any Punch or Kick
Air Double	↓↘→ + any Punch
Pressure Move	→ + FK

27

Mario Kart 64
The Characters

KOOPA

Bowser is one of the biggest characters in Mario Kart 64 and this gives him obvious advantages, but it also provides one major disadvantage. The King Koopa's speed is excellent, and his high body weight means that his kart can hold the racing line extremely well. However, Bowser's acceleration rate is poor, this is a direct result of his excess weight.

His speed and turning ability make Bowser a good character to choose once you can skillfully control the kart—however, novice players may find his lack of acceleration too much to deal with!

DONKEY KONG

Donkey Kong is almost identical in terms of ability to Bowser—both characters have a high top speed and great handling, but are let down by poor acceleration. This makes him more suited to more experienced players.

The problem is that if you keep crashing into the walls and obstacles, you'll find his lack of acceleration will really have a detrimental effect on your position—the key is to keep your speed high and use Kong's cornering ability to stay ahead of your opponent.

LUIGI

As you should be able to tell by looking at his statistics, Luigi is a good all-around character. His top speed and acceleration are both fairly good, and his turning ability is also slightly above average.

These three factors added together mean that he's among the best characters in the game to race.

This is also the first time Mario's brother has made an appearance on the Nintendo 64!

MARIO

Mario is, as you would expect, almost identical to his younger brother Luigi, and this means that he's another character who is good at everything, but exceptional at nothing. Mario is a perfect character to choose when you're just starting to play the game. His speed and turning ability make him the ideal choice for the novice, but he has enough scope to make him a good choice for the more advanced player too.

KINOPIO/TOAD

Toad is a small character who relies on acceleration rather than top speed. His ability to get the "fast start" is much better than the other characters, but unfortunately his top speed is relatively low. This means that he has problems holding onto any advantage he gains. Another of Toad's problems is due to his size, or rather lack of it! Because he is so small Toad gets bumped around by the other characters, making it all too easy to spin off. Toad is recommended for novice players.

PEACH/PRINCESS

The light-weight Princess has good acceleration and an above average top speed, but her lack of weight means that her turning ability is poor—this makes cornering very difficult, particularly on the faster courses. For these reasons the Princess is only recommended to the more experienced Mario Kart player, as a novice may find her lack of maneuverability too much to cope with.

WARIO

Wario is new to the ranks of Mario Kart and he certainly makes an impression. Mario's nemesis is probably one of the best characters in the game! Wario has a good top speed, slightly above average acceleration, and good turning ability. All this adds up to a character who is perfect for novice and expert players alike.

Another reason Wario is so good is that unlike the smaller characters, like Toad, his size means he won't get bumped from the course by the more aggressive-minded drivers. All-in-all Wario is a force to be reckoned with in Mario Kart 64.

YOSHI

Yoshi gets most people's vote as the second-best character in the game behind Wario. The two have almost identical statistics but Yoshi is a slightly smaller character than Wario, and this means he tends to get knocked around much more by the other racers. Basically, if you're playing in two-player mode and your buddy chooses Wario, make sure you go for Yoshi!

Power-Ups

Single Green Shell

You can drop these behind your kart by pushing back on the control stick and pressing the "use weapon" button. If you fire a single green shell forward, be careful—they can easily bounce back and hit you!

Triple Green Shell

This is a very useful power-up. Three green shells begin to circle your kart; now if any opponent gets too close they will be knocked flying off the track. The triple green shells cannot be dropped behind your kart.

Single Red Shell

The single red shell is similar than the green shell, but has one obvious advantage—it hones in. This biggest plus point is that the red shell will rarely bounce back and hit you, making it perfect for firing in an enclosed space.

Triple Red Shell

Similar to the triple green shells, three red shells will circle your kart and, if an opponent touches them, you'll get a hit! They can also be used to attack an opponent in front of you because they hone in when sent flying from your kart.

Single Banana

This gives you a single banana that you can drop behind your kart in an attempt to trip up one of you opponents. However, it is possible to throw the bananas forward by holding forward on the control stick and then pushing the attack button. When using this trick, make sure you don't slip on your own banana.

Bunch of Bananas

This power-up works in the same way as the single banana, the only difference is that you get five bananas for the price of one. This means you can lay traps and make it almost impossible for your opponents to pass unscathed!

Single Mushroom

No Mario game would be complete with mushrooms—a bit like a pizza really! This power-up gives your kart a sudden burst of speed, great for fast finishes or catching up an opponent after a crash.

Triple Mushroom

The same as the single mushroom, you just get three bursts of speed for the price of one—this power-up can turn the tide of a game in a matter of seconds.

Timed Mushroom

This golden mushroom power-up is very useful, it gives you an infinite power burst for a set amount of time. The time starts from the first time you use the power-up and lasts for about 15 seconds.

Giant Blue Shell

This all-powerful pick-up homes in on every opponent in front of you. Unlike the red shell, this power-up can take out more than one opponent at a time and is perfect for fighting your way to the front after a crash.

Thunder Flash

This is possibly the most useful power-up in Mario Kart 64. It turns all of the other seven competitors into miniature versions of themselves. They can only drive at half their usual speed and can be crushed as you overhaul them.

Invincibility Star

The invincibility star is fairly self-explanatory: For a set period of time your kart will be invulnerable to all attacks, even the Thunder Flash! You are not only invincible, but you can travel at twice the normal speed.

General Tips

● Getting a fast start can really put you in a good position to win your race; it also means that you won't get knocked around by your competitors in the early stages! As the starter floats down in his cloud, watch the lights carefully— as the lights begin to change, wait for the middle (blue) light to come on. At this point push and hold the accelerator, and keep the button held down until the race starts. If you've got it just right, you'll blast away from the start, leaving everyone behind. You can also use this cheat when being put back on the track after a crash—that will surprise your buddies!

● The shoulder buttons can be used to make your kart jump ever so slightly and, while this may seem pointless, it can be used to improve your lap time by a little. As you approach a corner, use the jump features to begin the turn and, as you land, your kart will be in a position to make the turn. This will mean you'll lose speed and turn more quickly.

● Don't worry if you are stuck in eighth place as the final lap starts. As stupid as it sounds, it is almost better to be out of the top three until the final few corners. The thing is that when you are at the front of the race you only receive low class power-ups—things like Single Green Shells and Bananas. These aren't much use to anyone. However, a character who is positioned outside the top four will receive lots of good pick-ups like Invincibility Stars and Thunder Flashes. This tactic will allow you to win the race and take out some of your competitors at the same time.

The Courses
Mushroom Cup

Luigi Circuit

This is the first track of Mario Kart 64 and to say it's easy is something of an understatement. The racing surface is made of asphalt, so grip is not a problem. The corners are banked making it possible to keep your speed high while taking the turns. The only area of the track that may cause you a few problems is the tunneled section—it's all too easy to get bounced around by your opponents in here, so take extra care. Other than this small problem, Luigi Circuit is dead easy and represents nine guaranteed points.

Moh Moh Farm

This track is set around a small farm that comes complete with cartoon cows! The track is very dusty, so cornering can be a real problem, particularly for the smaller characters who have less weight and therefore less traction. Moles, who inhabit various sections of the raceway, can also cause problems. The key is to memorize where on the track these pesky little vermin are, and avoid them at all costs. Hitting one will send your kart flying uncontrollably into the air! The only other section to watch out for is near the start/finish line. The track goes under a small bridge where it's all too easy to hit one of the pillars that bar the track, so choose your line early and stick to it!

Noko Noko Beach

This course looks very similar to a track that featured in the original Mario Kart on the Super Nintendo. Because the race takes place on sand, getting enough grip to take the sharp corners at full speed is a real problem—in fact it's impossible for the small racers!

The Noko Noko Beach course features a number of ramps dotted around the raceway that can be used to reach the power-up blocks. The track is also the first one to feature a short cut; however, you'll need a mushroom speed-up to use it. After you've covered about half the track you'll come to a section featuring a group of ramps; the final ramp of the sequence is thinner than the others and points directly toward a nearby cave. As you go up the ramp use the speed-up, you'll jump into the small cave and be able to drive right through—this cuts out about half the track and guarantees victory!

Kara Kara Desert

This course may be the final track of the Mushroom Cup, but it's actually one of the easiest. As the course is set in the middle of a desert, the racing surface is loose and tricky to grip. Another problem that this course offers is the railroad that runs through the middle of the race track. At two sections you must cross the railroad—taking your life in your hands! You are better off stopping and waiting for the train to go past rather than attempting to rush past and get caught out. Other than this Kara Kara Desert, you should have no other problems at all! You can actually go along the tracks and drive through the railroad tunnel the train comes from, but by doing this you fail to cross the checkpoint line, so there's no point—except for novelty value.

Flower Cup
Kinopio Highway

This track is by far the most difficult up to this point. As its name suggests this course is set on a large freeway complete with cars, huge trucks, and even school buses that tower above the karts as they race around the "figure of 8" circuit! While the traffic on this stage causes all manner of problems, the actual racing surface is asphalt so grip is not a problem—and when you're trying to avoid huge trucks this is a valuable thing to have on your side!

The only other thing to bear in mind while racing this track is that all the power-ups are found on the left side of the track in a pull-in, always consider your positioning as you race toward them. It's no good dashing across three lanes of traffic at the last minute to grab a power-up, you'll end up as road kill every time. The key is to think ahead!

Frappe Snowland

This track is set in the picturesque Frappe Snowlands, however while this makes for great scenery it certainly gives you plenty of racing problems. Getting grip to take the corners at anything like top speed is almost impossible, so this is where your ability to "jump" into a corner really starts to come good—check out the "general tips" section if you don't know how to use this brilliant little trick!

The other major problem that this track throws at you comes in the form of mini snowmen. These annoying little guys are dotted around the track—usually on the racing line, so they cause maximum confusion! All you can do is use the first lap to build up a picture in your head of where the snowmen are, then use this information to avoid them on later laps.

Choco Mountain

 This twisty course is set around a large, fog covered mountain and the lack of visibility coupled with the dusty racing surface makes it a tricky one. The first section is narro and twisty, and should be taken at full speed—even if you lose traction. The walls surrounding the track mean that you can't come to any harm. The track now enters a short tunneled section—watch out for banana skins through here, as crashing proves to be all too easy. Now you enter the final section of the course—and the most difficult. The track bears sharply to the left and takes you past a rock fall; these huge boulders crush anyone foolish enough to get too close. The trick is to stay to the far right of the track, while keeping your eyes open for falling rocks. Not easy!

Mario Circuit

The final circuit of the Flower Cup, is very similar to the Luigi track you raced on earlier. The course surface is asphalt, so grip is not a problem, even for the small racers. However, this isn't to say that Mario Circuit is easy—lots of sharp bends and twisty corners make this course a real test. Another factor to cause problems on the track is that the CPU controlled karts are never more than a couple of inches behind you—this means that even the slightest mistake can cost you a place in the top four. The key is to anticipate the corners and to stay on the racing line—go off the track, and you'll lose time and speed, something you don't have on a fast course like this. Fall behind your opponents too far, and getting back into the ranking is almost impossible!

Star Cup
Wario Stadium

This is the first track of the Star Cup, but is actually one of the easiest so far. Basically the course is an indoor Motocross circuit, so you don't have to worry about things like crashing off the track, falling rocks, little snowmen, or fog! The key to this track is to keep your speed high, anticipate the corners early, and stay ahead of your rivals! This course represents the perfect start to what is quite a tricky championship—get nine points here, and you're well on the way to winning the Star Cup!

Sherbert Land

This is the second course to be set in sub-zero conditions, and if you thought that Frappe Snowland was difficult, Sherbert Land will have you shaking in your boots—the racing surface is actually ice! So, as you can imagine, grip is pretty much non-existent. If you're controlling one of the smaller characters, like Toad or the Princess, you're going to be in for a tough time!

Another problem comes in the form of the huge lake you're racing around. A number of corners are unprotected and a mistake by even the slightest of margins will have you crashing into the freezing water, losing you lots of time. Use the "jump" cornering technique as outlined in the "general tips" section to make life a little easier. Use this in conjunction with good anticipation, so you're ready for the corner before it happens—and you might just make it around in one piece!

Peach Circuit

This course is the Princess' track (she's called Peach in Japan) and is very similar to the course that bears the name of Mario and his brother Luigi. With asphalt for the track surface, grip is not a problem, and the length of the circuit makes it possible to win the race even when starting the final lap from last position!

Most of the corners are sweeping and prove easy to take at full speed—even for the small competitors.

The middle section of the track features a huge jump that sends your kart soaring into the air, two large speed-up pads can be found just before the jump and are essential to clear it safely. You must not crash while approaching this jump as your kart's speed alone is not enough to make it across in one piece. The final section of the circuit is very twisty, with a lake to the one side. You must stay on the racing line while taking these corners as leaving the track will almost certainly result in your ending up in the water! This is a difficult course but still represents a good opportunity to take nine points.

Bowser's Castle

The final course of the Star Cup and Bowser's Castle is by far the hardest track you'll have come up against so far. The lap begins outside the castle and is fairly easy; however, before long the track takes you inside, and this is where the problems start! Huge stomping blocks can be found all over the track, they rise then crash down onto the racing line, crushing any kart that gets too close—you must avoid these at all costs!

With this section out of the way you enter a courtyard section of the track. Large bushes line either side of the racing line, and deviation results in a nasty crash. You now exit the castle and at this point things get a little easier, after a complete turn of 360° you must make a jump over a lava pit. Keep the kart straight and your speed high, falling into the lava below is a mistake from which it is almost impossible to recover. With that done, all that remains is to make the final turn and cross the start/finish line. This track is very difficult, and getting nine points on anything above 100CC speed level is extremely tough, to say the least. For this reason it's a good idea to use the first three races to build up a gap in the championship, this means that you won't have to come first and it also takes off some of the pressure!

Special Cup
Donkey Kong Jungle

This first race of the Special Cup is not for the faint-hearted. Twisty turns and tricky tunnel sections make this course a tough place to start your championship campaign.
The first section of the lap is by far the easiest, stay on the

racing line and away from the river, fall in and your race will be over before it's begun!

You must now make a huge jump across the river. Once again a large speed-up pad proceeds the jump, so use this to gain the required speed. You now enter a dense jungle section that twists one way, then the next. It is essential to stay on the track while racing through this section as you'll be bombarded with coconuts should you leave the racing line! Now the track drops down and heads across a thin rope bridge. This narrow section is the perfect place to use any banana power-ups, and avoiding them is almost impossible.

You now enter the final section of the lap, it takes you through a large cave. Power-ups can be found to the side of the track, so grab one of these. After a small incline, you'll find yourself crossing the finish line. This course is difficult, but not impossible. Hold your nerve, use your power-ups wisely, and victory can be yours!

Yoshi Canyon

This is probably the hardest track in the entire game, so pulling out a win here is a real achievement. The lap starts off easy enough, but before long you'll enter the canyon section, and this is where things get tough! The track splits up into a number of different paths, each with its good and bad points; however, they have no barriers to protect you from a fall to the bottom of the canyon. You must use skillful control of the kart to get through here safely—remember it is better to slow down and stay on the track!

Other than that piece of advice, there is little else to say about getting through this section. There are about five different ways to choose and each has good and bad points—find one that suits you and stick with it. The more you use the same route, the more skillfully you'll be able to drive it. The final section of the track takes you past a huge egg, which crushes anyone who gets too close, so once again it's better to slow down and get past safely. After a short uphill section you come back to the start/finish line.

Ghost House

This is another course that makes a return to the original Mario Kart on the Super Nintendo, albeit in a much more impressive form. The first section takes place outside on an old timber causeway, however about halfway around the lap you enter the ghost house itself. Once you enter this section, follow the giant arrows painted on the walls that indicate you the route you must take. This track is probably the fastest in the game but isn't without its problems. Large sections of the course are unprotected, and falling off is all too easy. Use careful control of your kart to stay on the racing line. Fall off, and you'll end up in the water below, losing you lots of time. A top-three finish on this course is a good effort.

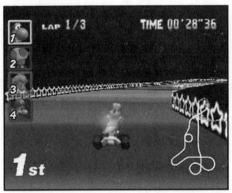

Rainbow Road

The final track in Mario Kart 64 is the legendary Rainbow Road, and those of you who played the original version on the Super Nintendo should have fond memories of this baby. However, unlike the Super Nintendo incarnation, this time around Rainbow Road is a whole lot easier. A star fence surrounds the race area, making it impossible to fall off, something that was always a big problem on the 16-bit version.

The biggest problem Rainbow Road poses comes in the form of giant bomb creatures that "eat" their way through the track—hit one of these and you crash, big time! However, the length of the course—it's by far the longest in the game—means that almost any gap can be recovered and a few good power-ups can take you from last to first in a matter of seconds! Winning Rainbow Road on any CC level shouldn't be that tough, and will give you a good chance to finish the championship on a high!

Mortal Kombat Trilogy

Play as Shao Kahn

Choose any character from the selection screen, and then enter either the Pit 3 or Rooftop stage. Now before the round starts press and hold **D, HP,** and **LP.**

Your chosen character will explode and Shao Kahn will replace him ready to fight. The only snag is that if you win the game will default back to the original character you chose for the rest of the battle.

Play as Motaro

Choose any character and go to either the Jade's Desert, Kahn's Tower, or The Wasteland stages. Now before the round starts press and hold **B, HK,** and **LK.**

Another explosion will swap your character for Motaro. Again, the game will default back to your chosen character if you win the fight.

Special Moves for the Boss Characters

Motaro

Special moves

Grab & punch	→ → → HP
Teleport	↓ ← HK
Fireball	Hold LK

Shao Kahn

Special moves

Laugh	↓ ↓ Run
Taunt	Hold Block ↑ ↑ Run
Laser Ball	→ ↓ → LK
Head Hammer	→ ← ← HP
Shoulder Charge	→ → HP
Shoulder Uppercut	↓ ↓ → HK

Finishing moves

Fatality 1	→ → ← HP (Jump)

Uncover the Blue ? Block

On the story line screen press these buttons quickly:
Run, Block, Block, Run, HP, LP.

If you've done it correctly, you will hear "Outstanding."
Now press the **Start** button and cycle through the icons to
find a new blue question mark block. Open this up and
you'll find...

Level Select
Throwing
Unlimited Run
Bloody Kombat
Smoke
Chameleon

If you select Smoke and Chameleon to be on, they will now
be selectable from the character selection screen, replacing
the Dragon symbols.

Babality Glitch

This isn't exactly a cheat, but it's an interesting bug in the
game that you can play with. Just tap **HP, LP, HK, LK**
immediately after performing a Babality move, but be quick
about it. Your foe will morph into a baby, then immediately
morph back into their fuller form, followed by an explosion.
The word **"FATALITY"** will appear instead of **"BABALITY"**
and the game will continue as normal. Strange!

Select a Background

On the character selection screen move to Sonya to
highlight her then press and hold the **Start** button and **Up**
together. You'll hear an explosion in the background.

Now choose your character, and you'll go to a
background selection screen before fighting.

Stage Select

Once the character selection screen has appeared, move
the selection box to Sonya's portrait. Now push **Up** on
the joypad and press the **Start** button. If you've done this
correctly, the screen will shake. Now, when both fighters
have been selected, you will be able to cycle through all
the battle arenas featured in the game and select your
favorite!

Special Moves
Key

LP	**Low Punch**
HP	**High Punch**
LK	**Low Kick**
HK	**High Kick**
Block	**Block**
Run	**Run**

Baraka
Special moves

Shredder	← ← ← LP
Spark	↓ ← HP
Swipe	← HP

Finishing moves

Fatality 1	← ← ← HP (Sweep)
Fatality 2	← → ↓ → LP (Sweep)
Friendship	↓ → → HK (Any)
Babality	→ → → HK (Any)
Pit Fatality	LK Run Run Run Run (Close)
Animality	Hold HP → ← ↓ → (Close)
Brutality	HP HP LP Block HK HK LK LK Block (Close)

Johnny Cage
Special moves

Hi Fireball	→ ↓ ← HP
Low Fireball	← ↓ → LP
Punch Uppercut	← ↓ ← HP
Shadow Kick	← → LK

Finishing moves

Fatality 1	↓ ↓ → → LP (Close)
Fatality 2	↓ ↓ → LK (Close)
Friendship	↓ ↓ ↓ ↓ LK (Any)
Babality	→ ← ← HK (Any)
Pit Fatality	↓ ← → → Block (Close)
Animality	↓ → → → HK Block (Close)
Brutality	LK HK LP HP HK HK HP HP LP HP (Close)

Classic Sub-Zero
Special moves

Ice Ball	↓ → + LP
Ice Shower	↓ → + HP
Sub Clone	↓ ← + LP
Ninja Slide	← + LP + Block + LK
Ice Ball	↓ → + LP
Ground Ice	↓ ← LK
Ninja Slide	← + LP + Block + LK

Finishing moves

Fatality 1	↓ ↓ ↓ → HP (Close)
Fatality 2	↓ → → → HP (Close)
Friendship	↓ ← ← → LK (Sweep)
Babality	↓ ← ← HK (Any)
Pit Fatality	→ ↓ → → HP (Close)
Animality	← ← → ↓ LP (Close)
Brutality	LP HP Block LK LK HK HK LP HP LP (Close)

Cyrax
Special moves

Net	← ← LK
Short Bomb	Hold LK ← ← HK
Long Bomb	Hold LK → → HK
Air Throw	→ ↓ → + Block LP
Teleport	→ ↓ + Block

Finishing moves

Fatality 1	↓ ↓ ↑ ↓ HP (Close)
Fatality 2	↓ ↓ → ↑ Run (Close)
Friendship	Run Run Run ↑ (Sweep)
Babality	→ → ← HP (Any)

Pit Fatality	Run Block Run (Close)
Animality	↑ ↑ ↓ ↓ (Close)
Brutality	HK HP HK HK HP HK HP
	HK LK LP(Close)

Ermac
Special moves
Fireball	↓ ← LP
T. Punch	↓ ← HP
T. Slam	← ↓ ← HK

Finishing moves
Fatality 1	Run Block Run Run HK (Close)
Fatality 2	↓ ↑ ↓ ↓ ↓ Block (Close)
Friendship	→ → → HP (Sweep)
Babality	↓ ↓ ← ← HP (Any)
Pit Fatality	Run Run Run Run LK (Close)
Animality	← ← → → LK (Close)
Brutality	HP LP Block HK LK Block
	HP LP LK HK

Human Smoke
Special moves
| Teleport Punch | ↓ ← HP |
| Stun Spear | ← ← LP |

Finishing moves
Fatality 1	→ → ← Run (Sweep)
Fatality 2	Run Block Run Run HK (Sweep)
Friendship	↓ → → → Run (Sweep)
Babality	← ← → Run (Any)
Pit Fatality	→ ↑ ↑ LP (Close)
Animality	→ → → ← HK (Close)
Brutality	HP Block LK HK HP HK HP
	HK LP LK (Close)

Jade
Special moves
Shureken Middle	← → LP
Shureken High	← → HP
Shureken Low	← → LK
Invincibility	← → HK
Glow Kick	↓ → LK

Finishing moves

Fatality 1	↑ ↑ ↓ → HP (Close)
Fatality 2	Run Run Run Block Run (Close)
Friendship	← ↓ ← ← HK (Far)
Babality	↓ ↓ → ↓ HK (Any)
Pit Fatality	← → ↓ Run (Close)
Animality	→ ↓ → → LK (Sweep)
Brutality	LK HP LP HK HK LK
	Block Block HP HK

Jax

Special moves

Missile Shot	← → HP
Double Missile Shot	→ → ← ← HP
Dash Punch	→ → HK
Gotcha Grab	→ → LP (x5)
Ground Pound	(LK) 3 seconds
Back Breaker	Block (In Air)

Finishing moves

Fatality 1	Block (↑ ↓ → ↑) (Close)
Fatality 2	Run Block Run Run LK (Full Screen)
Friendship	LK Run Run LK (Far)
Babality	↓ ↓ ↓ LK (Any)
Pit Fatality	↓ → ↓ LP (Close)
Animality	(LP) → → ↓ → (Close)
Brutality	HP HP Block LP HP HP
	HP Block LP HP (Close)

Kabal

Special moves

Fireball	← ← HP
Air Ball	← ← HP (in Midair)

| Web Spin | ← → + LK |
| Ground Saw | ← ← ← Run |

Finishing moves

Fatality 1	↓ ↓ ← → Block (Outside Sweep)
Fatality 2	Run Block Block Block HK (Close)
Friendship	Run LK Run Run ↑ (Sweep)
Babality	Run Run LK (Any)
Pit Fatality	Block Block HK (Close)
Animality	HP (→ → ↓ →) (Close)
Brutality	Block LK LK LK HK LP LP
	LP HP LP (Close)

Kano
Special moves

Horizontal Ball	(LK) 3 seconds
Blade Toss	↓ ← + HP
Blade Swipe	↓ → + HP
Grab & Bite	↓ → + LP
Air Throw	Block (In Air)
Rising Ball	→ ↓ → + HK

Finishing moves

Fatality 1	LP (→ ↓ ↓ →) (Close)
Fatality 2	LP Block Block HK (Sweep)
Friendship	LK Run Run HK (Sweep)
Babality	→ → ↓ ↓ LK (Any)
Pit Fatality	U U ← LK (Close)
Animality	HP (Block Block Block) (Close)
Brutality	LP Block LP HP Block
	HK LK Block HK LK

Kitana
Special moves

Fan Toss	→ → HP + LP
Fan Lift	← ← ← HP
Warp Punch	↓ ← HP

Finishing moves

Fatality 1	Run Run Block Block LK (Close)
Fatality 2	← ↓ → → HK (Close)
Friendship	↓ ← → → LP (Sweep)

Babality	→ → ↓ → HK (Any)
Pit Fatality	→ ↓ ↓ LK (Close)
Animality	↓ ↓ ↓ ↓ Run (Inside Sweep)
Brutality	HP Block HK Block LK Block LP Block HP Block

Kung Lao

Special moves

Hat Throw	← → LP
Teleport	↓ ↑
Whirlwind Spin	→ ↓ → + Run
Dive Kick	↓ + HK (In Air)

Finishing moves

Fatality 1	Run Block Run Block ↓ (Far)
Fatality 2	→ → ← ↓ HP (Inside Sweep)
Friendship	Run LP Run LK (Past Sweep)
Babality	↓ → → HP (Any)
Pit Fatality	↓ ↓ → → LK (Close)
Animality	Run Run Run Run Block (Close)
Brutality	LP LK HK Block HP LP LK HK Block HP

Liu Kang

Special moves

High Fireball	→ → + HP
Low Fireball	→ → + LP
Bicycle Kick	(LK) 3 Seconds
Flying Kick	→ → HK

Finishing moves

Fatality 1	→ → ↓ ↓ LK (Any)
Fatality 2	↑ ↓ ↑ ↑ Block + Run (Any)
Friendship	Run Run Run ↓ + Run (Sweep)
Babality	↓ ↓ ↓ HK (Any)
Pit Fatality	Run Block Block LK (Close)
Animality	↓ ↓ ↑ (Sweep)
Brutality	LP HP Block LK HK LK HK LP LP HP (Close)

Mileena

Special moves

Sai Toss	(HP) 2 Seconds
Teleport Kick	→ → LK
Ground Roll	← ← ↓ HK

Finishing moves

Fatality 1	← ← ← → LK (Full Screen)
Fatality 2	↓ → ↓ → LP (Close)
Friendship	↓ ↓ ← → HP (Far)
Babality	↓ ↓ → → HP (Any)
Pit Fatality	↓ ↓ ↓ LP (Close)
Animality	→ ↓ ↓ → HK (Close)
Brutality	LP LP HP Block HK LK HK Block HP LP (Close)

Nightwolf

Special moves

Aura Arrow	↓ ← + LP
Axe Uppercut	↓ → + HP
Aura Repel	← ← ← + HK
Shadow Shoulder	→ → + LK

Finishing moves

Fatality 1	↑ ↑ ← → Block (Close)
Fatality 2	← ← ↓ HP (Half Screen)
Friendship	Run Run Run ↓ (Past Sweep)
Babality	→ ← → ← LP (Any)
Pit Fatality	Run Run Block (Close)
Animality	→ → ↓ ↓ (Close)
Brutality	HP HK LK LK Block Block LP LP HP HK (Close)

Noob Saibot

Special moves

Soul Blast	↓ → LP
Telethrow	↓ ↑
Alter Ego	→ → HP

Finishing moves

Fatality 1	← ← → → HK (Far)
Fatality 2	↓ ↓ ↑ Run (Any)
Friendship	→ → ← HP (Any)
Babality	→ → → LP (Any)
Pit Fatality	↓ → Block (Close)
Animality	← → ← → HK (Close)
Brutality	LK LP Block LK HK HP LP Block LK HK (Close)

Rain

Special moves

Super Round House	← HK
Storm Zap	↓ → HP
Light Bolt	← ← HP

Finishing moves

Fatality 1	→ → →↓ HP (Close)
Fatality 2	↓ ↓ ← → HK (Sweep)
Friendship	→ → → LP (Far)
Babality	→ ← ← HP (Any)
Pit Fatality	→ ↓ → LP (Close)
Animality	Block Block Run Run Block (Close)
Brutality	HP Block LK HK Block LK HK Block HP LP (Close)

Rayden

Special moves

Dive	← ← →
Teleport	↓ ↑
Zap Bolt	↓ → LP
Electrograb	(HP) 3 Seconds

Finishing moves

Fatality 1	Hold HK for 5 Seconds Tap LK/Block (Close)
Fatality 2	Hold HP for 5 Seconds (Close)
Friendship	↓ ← → HK (Far)
Babality	↓ ↓ ↑ ← (Any)
Pit Fatality	↓ ↓ ↓ HP (Close)
Animality	↓ → → HK (Close)
Brutality	HK LK LK LK HK LP LP LP Block Block (Close)

Reptile

Special moves

Acid Spit	→ → HP
Slow Force Ball	← ← HP + LP
Fast Force Ball	→ → HP + LP
Ninja Slide	← + LP + Block + LK
Invisibility	↑ ↓ HK
Dashing Elbow	← → LK

Finishing moves

Fatality 1	← → ↓ Block (Jump)
Fatality 2	→ → ↑ ↑ HK (Inside Sweep)
Friendship	↓ → → ← HK (Close)
Babality	→ → ← ↓ LK
Pit Fatality	Block Run Block Block

Animality	↓ ↓ ↓ ↑ HK (Close)
Brutality	Block HK HK Block HP LP LK LK
	Block LP (Close)

Scorpion
Special moves
Spear	← ← LP
Teleport Punch	↓ ← HP
Air Throw	Block in air

Finishing moves
Fatality 1	↓ ↓ ↑ HK (Jump)
Fatality 2	→ → ← LP (Jump)
Fatality 3	→ → ↓ ↑ Run (Close)
Friendship	← → → ← LK (Close)
Babality	↓ ← ← → HP (Any)
Pit Fatality	→ ↑ ↑ LP (Close)
Animality	→ ↑ ↑ HK (Close)
Brutality	HP Block HK HK LK HK HP HP LP
	HP (Close)

Sektor
Special moves
Missile	→ → LP
Hommer Missile	→ ↓ ← + HP
Teleport Uppercut	→ → LK

Finishing moves
Fatality 1	LP Run Run Block (Sweep)
Fatality 2	→ → → ← Block (Far)
Friendship	Run Run Run Run ↓ (Far)
Babality	← ↓ ↓ ↓ HK (Any)
Pit Fatality	Run Run Run ↓ (Close)
Animality	→ → ↓ ↑ (Close)
Brutality	HP Block Block HK HK
	LK LK LP LP HP

Sheeva
Special moves
Teleport Stomp	↓ ↑
Fireball	↓ → + HP
Ground Stomp	← ↓ ← HK

Finishing moves

Fatality 1	→ ↓ ↓ → LP (Close)
Fatality 2	HK (← → →) (Close)
Friendship	→ → ↓ → HP
Babality	↓ ↓ ↓ ← HK
Pit Fatality	↓ → ↓ → LP
Animality	Run Block Block Block Block (Close)
Brutality	LP Block LK HK Block HK LK Block LP HP (Close)

Sindel

Special moves

Shriek Wave	→ → → HP
Float	← ← → HK
Fireball	→ → LP
Air Fireball	↓ → + LK (In Air)

Finishing moves

Fatality 1	Run Run Block Run Block (Sweep)
Fatality 2	Run Block Block Run + Block (Close)
Friendship	Run Run Run Run Run ↑ (Far)
Babality	Run Run Run ↑ (Any)
Pit Fatality	↓ ↓ ↓ LP (Close)
Animality	→ → ↑ HP (Any)
Brutality	Block LK Block LK HK Block HK LK Block LP (Close)

Smoke

Special moves

Spear	← ← LP
Teleport Punch	→ → LK
Air Throw	Block in midair
Invisibility	↑ ↑ Run

Finishing moves

Fatality 1	Block (↑ ↑ → ↓) (Full Screen)
Fatality 2	Run + Block (↓ ↓ → ↑) (Sweep)
Friendship	Run Run Run HK (Full Screen)
Babality	↓ ↓ ← ← Block (Any)
Pit Fatality	→ → ↓ LK (Close)

Animality	↓ → → Block (Full Screen)
Brutality	LK LK HK Block Block LP LP HP
	Block Block (Close)

Sonya
Special moves
Ring Toss	↓ → LP
Leg Throw	↓ + LP + Block
Flying Punch	→ ← HP
Leg Kick	← ← ↓ HK

Finishing moves
Fatality 1	Block + Run (↑ ↑ ← ↓) (Far)
Fatality 2	← → ↓ ↓ Run (Far)
Friendship	← → ← ↓ Run (Sweep)
Babality	↓ ↓ → LK (Any)
Pit Fatality	→ → ↓ HP (Close)
Animality	LP (← → ↓ →) (Close)
Brutality	LK Block HP LK Block HP LP Block
	HK LK (Close)

Stryker
Special moves
Club Throw	→ → HK
Club Take Down	→ ← LP
Low Grenade	↓ ← + LP
High Grenade	↓ ← + HP
Gun Blast	← → + HP

Finishing moves
Fatality 1	↓ → ↓ → Block (Close)
Fatality 2	→ → → LK (Far)
Friendship	LP Run Run LP (Far)
Babality	↓ → → ← HP (Any)
Pit Fatality	→ ↑ ↑ HK (Close)
Animality	Run Run Run Block (Sweep)
Brutality	LP HK LK HP LP LK HK HP
	LK LK (Close)

Shadows of the Empire
Stage Tips

Battle of Hoth
Stage One

Objective: Destroy the four Imperial Probe Droids.

● Beware of running into the ground. This damages your ship and life's hard enough without having to fly a garbage can. If your viewscreen jumps a lot, either enemy shots are hitting you or your speeder's sucking snow drifts.

● Use your radar display to find targets out of your field of view.

● Try lining up a nearby target by flying away from it, then turning to face it from a distance. This technique gives you more shots per pass, critical for wreaking havoc in the later stages.

● Holding down the Fire button may give you a steady stream of shots, but pressing it repeatedly makes for more "Swiss" in the Empire's cheese.

● In the heat of battle, remember that your cockpit console's center display shows your current target's remaining hit points.

● To make a tighter turn, engage your brakes and pull hard in the direction you're turning. For even more "break-neck" turns, set the control setting to Traditional to control left and right brakes separately. (Engaging only the right brake when turning to the right, for example, tightens the turn significantly.)

Stage Two

Objective: Destroy the attacking forces (two AT-STs, two Droids).

- Keep the air brakes on during your attack run to lengthen your time on target.
- Begin your attack runs on AT-STs from a long way out. This buys you time to acquire and line up your target, and allows you to rifle more blaster rounds at them. Fly away from your victim until it's at the edge of your radar before coming around to scorch 'em on another pass.
- Remember, enemy units can't fire on what's behind them.
- Aim at the narrow rear portion of the AT-ST just between the legs and the head. This is the soft spot that will drop it to its knees the quickest.

Stage Three

Objective: Destroy the attacking forces (two AT-STs, two Droids, one AT-AT).

- If you must cross in front of an AT-AT, fly either very low and close, or very high.
- Watch your altitude while circling those Walkers. Try to fly at a constant height about even with their "knees." This keeps you off the snow and below the forward-facing blasters on its head.
- If you choose not to use the tow cable against the AT-ATs, then be sure to aim at the head, where your blasters will get the most bang for their buck.
- Unless you count their occasional complaints when they fly into your blaster path, the Snow Speeders flying with you are not much use but

to draw enemy fire. Don't count on your
wingmen to be much less than cannon fodder.

Stage Four

Objective: Destroy the attacking forces (four AT-STs, four
Droids, two AT-ATs).

● Long attack-run approaches let you see whether
another AT-ST or Probe Droid protects your
target; if so, you can select another target right
away without flying farther out to line it up.

● Using tow cables to destroy the AT-ATs earns
you Challenge Points. This battle's two Big
Walkers mean 2 bonus points are possible.

● Watch out for AT-STs covering each other. Don't
line up for a long, slow attack run on one AT-ST
if the other has you in its sights. Try to select a
target with an unprotected rear approach.

● Yes, you can fly between the AT-AT's legs, but it
serves no real purpose and is exceedingly
dangerous. (It may impress your
friends, however...)

Escape from the Echo Base

Stage One

Objective: Find your way through the base and
reactivate the power generators.

● The "over-your-shoulder" camera view lets you
guide Dash with better precision because you
can see where he's stepping and how close to
objects he is. It's worth the effort it takes to
adjust to this perspective. The only drawback is
that the camera moves a little slower than Dash

when he turns a corner; you could walk into Imperial troops and not realize it until the camera catches up. Strafing around corners solves this problem.

- The number of Imperial Stormtroopers and the accuracy with which they fire depends on your difficulty setting, but even at the Easy setting a few choice shots at close range can easily buy you a casket.
- Be sure to shoot and destroy all boxes and crates on these levels. They often contain health, weapons, and even free lives.

Stage Two

Objective: Find your way through the base and reactivate the power generators.

- Two of the four turbines hold challenge points. As you enter the turbine room the challenge points are in the right-hand unit and the turbine diagonal to it.
- In the generator section, before going up the lift you should collect the challenge points and free lives behind the last two turbines. Although it's possible to get these items when the generator is running, it's considerably more challenging!

Asteroid Chase

Stage One

Objective: Destroy all TIE bombers and TIE fighters in the asteroid field. Break up the six challenge-point asteroids.

● It's easier to line up your targets using the "from-the-cockpit" view. The exterior view gives you a cone of fire but it's difficult to aim accurately.

● You'll see six red asteroids during your battle. Turn them to dust to earn challenge points.

● Your order of targeting priority should be 1. TIE bombs and bombers; 2. red asteroids; 3. TIE fighters.

● Don't be afraid to use your missiles. These babies are highly effective and will reload in a fairly short period. There's no limit to how many missiles you can reload.

● In cockpit mode, constantly turning your ship provides a full 360-degree view. Check your "six" frequently to avoid getting rocked in the back by plasma bombs.

Ord Mantell Junkyard

Stage One

Objective: Ride the train successfully all the way to the junkyard, where you'll meet IG-88.

- Get out your old high school science texts because the physics on these trains is all too real. If you jump in the air while the train makes a sharp turn, centrifugal force affects your arc. You can fly right off the train if you're not careful! You'll notice these forces when you're trying to walk along the length of the train. Measured hysteria is the best way to make it through the trains without missing jumps.
- If you jump slightly in the direction of the turn you should land where you want. Don't worry if you bite the dust a couple of times in this level. There are several free lives to be had.
- Shoot the droids as they come into view. Generally they'll blow up after taking one decent direct hit, and if you don't get rid of them they'll harass you to no end.

Stage Two

Objective: Destroy IG-88.

- Seekers are the most powerful ranged weapon at your disposal, but they don't lock onto IG-88, so your aiming accuracy is crucial.
- Unfortunately, there's a scarcity of Health power-ups in the junkyard building, so your best defense is to keep moving and avoid IG-88 until he's lined up in your sights.
- The platforms above the floor at either end of this room provide the best vantage point to see IG-88 approach and to fire from.

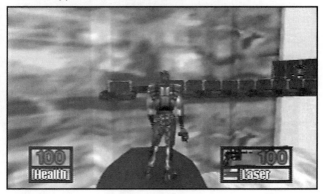

Gall Spaceport

Stage One

Objective: After you leave your ship you're in for some nail-biting cliff-walking.

● Overhead view is often best for negotiating those precarious ledges. Switch to over-the-shoulder view to line up the jump and see where your feet are stepping as you land.

● When you enter the base it's best to peek around the corner and expose yourself to one Laser Cannon at a time to avoid taking too many hits.

● The key to using the jet pack is not to use the thruster unless you absolutely must. When flying from high to low, just push the stick forward and guide Dash in, using thrust only to gain height if needed. As you hop through the canyon, you can jump from pillar to pillar and land safely with 30–40 percent of your fuel every time.

● If you want to forego the challenge point in the pillar area, jumping to Pillar 3, then to Pillar 5 saves you two steps. This requires slightly better fuel conservation skills but saves you considerable time.

Stage Two

Objective: Work your way through the base and face off against an AT-ST and Boba Fett.

● There's a couple of challenge points to be had when you face Boba Fett. If you leave the "arena" you're fighting in and explore the external arena, you'll find some nice goodies. Best of all, neither Boba nor this ship will bother you while you're out there.

● When you use the jet pack, take a running jump before you take off. Turn on the jet pack as you reach the apex of your jump to buy yourself a little fuel.
Sometimes this little bit makes a big difference.

- Seekers won't track Boba Fett, so don't waste the ammo. Try to gun him down with your Laser or Pulse Cannon (if he's close by).

Mos Eisley and Beggar's Canyon

Stage One

Objective: Kill off the Swoop gang and make it to Ben Kenobi's hut.

- Although it's fun, in this stage speed isn't crucial. You need only keep up with the other riders. After all, if you hit an obstacle going too fast, you meet your maker.
- Kill off the Swoop gang first; then return to search for goodies and challenge points.

- Use narrow passageways to your advantage. Get close to the enemies and ram them into the cold, hard stone when crossing through an archway or tunnel.

Imperial Freighter Suprosa

Stage One

Objective: Make it through this section of the Freighter en route to the supercomputer.

- Be sure to check out all the crew quarters for goodies such as health, weapons, and invincibility.
- The challenge points are in relatively easy locations, but they're covered by many enemies.

Stage Two

Objective: Make it through this section of the Freighter en route to the supercomputer.

- Don't panic on the rotating tables. If necessary, stay and do a little extra jump-and-duck to get the hang of it.

● Use your Seekers to take out any enemies hiding behind obstacles. A Seeker can do in one second what a Blaster can do in four.

Stage Three
Objective: Make it through the level and get the supercomputer.
● When fighting the loader droid, back away from it and move from corner to corner. This should prevent you from taking any damage while you fight it off.

Sewers of Imperial City
Stage One
Objective: You must walk, swim, fly, and jump through the sewer system to find Xizor's lair.
● When battling a dianoga, remember that you can surface into the thin region of air at the top of the room when your air supply runs low. Doing this reduces your visibility somewhat (because you've surfaced).
● Don't let the whirlpool current drag you down into the Giant dianoga's mouth at the bottom of the room.
● When swimming underwater, keep an eye on your oxygen level. You don't want to get trapped where you can't surface for a breath of, well, "fresh" air.

Xizor's Palace
Stage One
Objective: Find your way through the palace to the three power couplings on the Skyhook connecting column. Place charges and get out again. On your way out you face the gladiator droid.
● At this stage of the game it pays off to explore anywhere you can. That includes jumping off bridges and having a look around. At the very least you'll pick up some more health, and maybe you'll even get to kill something.

- In these higher levels, tougher, more aggressive guards and droids fill all the rooms, so stay frosty or it'll be "Game Over," man.
- When moving around hallways near the bridges, use the pillars as cover as you slowly move forward.

Stage Two
Objective: Continue finding your way through the palace to the three power couplings on the Skyhook connecting column. Place charges and get out again. On your way out you'll face the gladiator droid.

- Whenever you're unsure of a jump or are afraid of falling, use your jet pack. If you fall, just turn on the pack to stabilize.
- A notch in the Skyhook shaft below the lowest power coupling holds a challenge point.
- Hit the gladiator dead-on with Disrupters. These are your most powerful weapons, and can save your life when you battle this foe.

Skyhook Battle
Stage One
Objective: Your first task is to use the Outrider's Blaster Turrets to clear away as many of Xizor's fighters as you can. Second, you must destroy four Laser Turrets on the arms of the Skyhook station. Third, you must fly into the Skyhook and destroy all four sides of the power reactor within.
- As you approach Skyhook, you can gain extra lives by destroying enemy spacecraft: For every 20 ships you destroy, you get a free life, so at the very least you should break even in the first space battle.
- Don't be afraid to use your missiles. They're renewable and can take out a couple of enemy ships at a time. When it comes to the final assault on the core, missiles are downright essential.

Wave Race 64
Fast Start

On the start line it is possible to get a fast start and give yourself maximum power to boot! As the announcer counters down, "Three, two, one, go"—push the accelerator at the exact moment he says "go!" You shoot off into the lead and have maximum power!

Ride the Dolphin

Go to "Stunt Mode" and select Dolphin Park. You must now ride through all of the rings on the course and then do the following tricks—in the correct order!

- Handstand
- Backward Spin
- Stand with Backflip
- Single Backflip off ramp
- Dive off ramp
- Barrel roll off ramp, in both directions

If you've performed the cheat correctly, you'll hear a squeaking sound as you cross the finishing line. Now, when you turn off the machine and go back to the title screen you'll see people riding on dolphins! In order to use the dolphin in a race, first select either Championship or Normal mode. Now on the analogue stick, when selecting your racer, hold Down. You'll now ride a dolphin when racing at Dolphin Park!

The Courses

Course One
Sandy Beach

Location:	**Ocean**
Wave difficulty:	**Easy**
Course difficulty:	**Easy**

This first course is set around a small island and is basically an oval loop. The race takes place on the sea so you'll have to contend with some tricky waves, but it's nothing too difficult. From the start you must to go through two buoys, both are well spaced out and shouldn't cause any problems.

Try to stay as straight as possible while going past them which will keep your speed as high as possible.

The course now turns sharply to the left; the trick here is to turn your craft as gently as possible. Force the turn, and you'll dip the front of the Jet Ski and lose speed. You are now on a long straightaway and you must navigate a series of buoys: first left, then right, then left, then finally back to the right. Take care as you approach the second left turn as a group of water-mines is hidden by the waves and hitting any of them will cause you to fall off your craft. With this section safely finished, you must make a sharp turn to the right, once again make the turn as smooth as possible.

You are now back on the start/finish straight, and two more buoys must be safely passed—they are well spaced out and easy to take at full speed. All that remains is to cross the finish line!

Course Two
Sunset Bay

Location: **Ocean**
Wave difficulty: **Easy**
Course difficulty: **Medium**
This second course is set at sunset and gives the ocean a deep, orange look—it's kinda' like racing in a sea of Orangeade! The waves are a little more troublesome than on the first course but still nothing to worry about. From the start you'll have to go round a couple of buoys, one to the left then other to the right—they are both well spaced out and can easily be taken at full speed. You must now make a tight left-hand corner and, as you make the turn, be sure you don't oversteer or you'll hit the wall!

You must now navigate two left buoys followed by one to the right; with this done you'll hit a ramp. Now, as you land, push back on the stick which will bring up the nose of the Jet Ski and avoid losing too much speed. With your landing taken care of, you must now go between two more buoys. The first is to the left, the second to the right, while both are spaced out, but the cross waves make controlling your craft difficult—feather the steering and stay in control!

The course now turns to the left. This isn't a sharp corner but oversteering will result in contact with the close-by wall, and this isn't a good idea! You must now make your way through a twisty section of buoys—they go left, right, then left again. The trick is to stay tight with the buoys and keep your Jet Ski as straight as possible, which will provide time to make corrections to your direction and, more importantly, keep your speed high. The course now bears to the left and enters the final section, a group of buoys follow—the sequence goes left, left, right, and then finally left. Take extra care as you pass the final buoy, because the course turns to the right while you are taking the buoy on the left side—it's easy to get this wrong. You are now back to the start/finish line!

Course Three
Misty Lake

Location: **Lake**
Wave difficulty: **No waves!**
Course difficulty: **Easy/Medium**

This course is a little different to the other courses featured in *Wave Race 64*. Rather than racing on the ocean, this race takes place on a huge lake! And that means you don't have to worry about your Jet Ski being thrown around by bobbing waves! However, while you don't suffer this headache, Misty Lake has an added problem—as its name suggests! When the race starts, thick fog makes the course barely visible; however, it only lasts for the first lap and a half, so hang in there!

From the start you go through a pair buoys, the first to the left the second to the right—keep the Jet Ski straight and keep your speed high. You must make a left turn; however, as you're taking this corner, "drift" your jetski away from the bank. This puts you in the perfect position to take the buoy that lies at the exit of this turn. A small island now splits the course, it doesn't really matter which path you take, as long as you choose your route early. Hit the island, and you'll lose all your momentum! Now the course turns sharply to the left onto a long straightaway and you must navigate a series of tightly spaced buoys.

The sequence goes left, right, left, right, and finally left—the trick is to set up your craft for the next turn as soon as possible, this means you won't have to make sudden directional changes. Now the course sweeps left, you'll go past the two buoys then enter a section of the course littered with stakes sticking out of the water. You must pick your way through these obstacles and go past the buoy that lies in the center. Now bear right and go around the final buoy; the start/finish straight lies directly in front of you.

Course Four
Marine Cause Way

Location: **Ocean**
Wave difficulty: **Hard**
Course difficulty: **Med**
This course features a shortcut that only becomes available after the first lap, when lots of debris appears in the water. You'll also have to cope with some of the biggest waves seen so far! From the start go forward, past the right buoy. Now, directly in front of you, a rock sticks out of the sea. You must either avoid this to the left or use the wave to "bounce" over it. The latter option is much harder and, to a certain extent, relies on luck; however, pull it off, and you'll get a nice head start.

Now you bear hard right to go between two more buoys, right, left, right—as you go past the third buoy, turn left sharply. The coming section has lots of debris in the water and the far left side of the course is the best way to avoid it. Now the course hangs another sharp right. Go past the two buoys on the right, followed by a hard left. On the second lap a gate will open at this point of the course and allow you to use a small short cut, use this when you get the chance. You'll now have to take a long corner to the right, it can easily be taken at full speed. You're now back on the start/finish straight.

Course Five
Urban Water Way

Location: **Ocean**
Wave difficulty: **Medium**
Course difficulty: **Medium**

This course features a very difficult short cut that can get
you out of trouble real quick; however, it requires skill and
nerve to hold the advantage. The waves on this course
are not quite as bad as the ones at Marine Causeway but
still throw you around badly! From the start, go straight,
two buoys will appear—one to the left, one to the right.
Simply go between these while accelerating. The course
now turns to the right. As you make this turn drift to the
left slightly, this puts you in the perfect position to go past
the two buoys that appear suddenly on the left. At this
point you have a choice: either take the longer, easy
route, or the shorter, hard route.

Easy Route: Head for the left-hand tunnel and go ahead.
As you exit the tunneled section, the course turns to the
right. This corner can be taken at full speed. You now enter
another, tunneled section, keep your craft pointed ahead
and gain maximum speed.

Hard Route: For the fast route you'll have to use the
second, smaller tunnel to the right. You are now in a
small, very twisty tunneled section—first it sweeps left,
then hard right, and then finally back to the left. This
section cuts down the distance you must travel by about
half, but you run the risk of hitting the wall—this'll cause
you to fall off your Jet Ski!

Both routes now join back together and the course hangs a sharp left. Stay wide on this corner—a couple of buoys can be found floating on the apex.

Now head directly forward and gain speed, you'll come to a jump. In the jump, steer right, which gives you an instant turn as you hit the water and puts you in the perfect position to attack the final straightaway. The start/finish line is dead ahead.

Course Six
Water City

Location: **Enclosed Ocean**
Wave difficulty: **Easy**
Course difficulty: **Medium**

The course is set around what appears to be a flooded city. It's night, and huge neon lights are everywhere. The water is almost motionless on this course, so at least you don't have to worry about avoiding 18-foot-high surf! From the start the course is straight, so use this section to build speed. Before long you'll come to a jump, stay in line and you'll make it across, no problem. When you land it seems as though you've jumped into a swimming pool section, and the course now enters a tunnel. As the tunnel ends, you'll have to make a sharp left-hand turn. As you make the turn, stay tight to the right wall—two buoys appear on the left, and if you're hugging the near side of the course, you'll get past them without having to worry at all!

Now the course goes ahead and over a jump. Make sure you hit the ramp because the water directly after the jump is littered with water mines and missing the ramp will mean you have to pick your way through these deadly devices!

Your next task is to get past a string of tightly spaced buoys—the sequence goes right, left, right, right, left, and left. Don't worry about this section too much, it sounds much harder than it actually is! Now you have to make two further jumps, both in quick succession—keep in line, and make sure you've got enough power to make both leaps comfortably! The course bears sharply left, and the start/finish line is dead ahead!

Course Seven Southern Island

Location:	**Ocean**
Wave difficulty:	**Easy**
Course difficulty:	**Difficult**

This course would be easy but for one feature that makes it different from all the others in *Wave Race 64*. You start this race with the tide in fully and this means the water level is high. However, as you complete your laps, the tide slowly goes out and, in the process, the water level drops. This means that obstacles covered over by water on the first lap are exposed by the third. Bear this is mind as you race this course!

From the start the course is straight, so use this section to build speed. The two buoys on this straightaway are easily passed. The course now turns to the left. Take care, as oversteering means you crash into the wall! You now enter a huge section of the course that offers lots of overhauling opportunities, this section will change from lap to lap as the tide goes out slowly. However, one thing remains the same—the order in which the buoys appear. The sequence goes right, left, right, left, and right. Remember this order, because no matter what this section

looks like, you must still pass the buoys on the correct side! The course now bears left, which brings you back onto the home straightaway. Two more buoys must be passed, so don't lose your concentration!
The finish line is dead ahead.

Course Eight
Icy Lake

Location: **Ocean**
Wave difficulty: **Medium**
Course difficulty: **Hard**

This course is set around a huge frozen island, and offers *Wave Race* experts the ultimate challenge! From the start, keep your Jet Ski straight, use this section to build your speed to a maximum. Use the ice ramps to pass the buoys lining either side of the straightaway—the sequence goes left, right, and left.

The course now turns sharply to the right as you enter a tight, ice-walled section—keep in line and avoid contact with the wall at all costs. You must make a difficult right-hand turn across the ice. The trick is to set up your Jet Ski for the turn before you actually get onto the ice. Now, as you slide across, don't make any directional changes. The course bears sharply right. Take this corner wide, as there are two right-hand buoys floating on the wide line of this corner. Now the course goes ahead and enters a section filled with ice blocks—again, avoid these at all costs.

Now you have to make another right-hand turn. This leads to a long straightaway that has a string of buoys. The sequence goes right, left, right, left, right, and right. As you move past the final buoy of the sequence, to make a right-hand turn. You are now back on the home straightaway.

Wayne Gretzky's 3D Hockey

General Tips

● Don't try to knock over the goal tender with a sly foul—it's usually the attacker who ends up flattened.

● Use your fouls wisely. Sending the opposition sprawling might be fun, but it doesn't score points.

● *Wayne Gretzky's* is ace with a few friends. Try a four-player, two-on-two game for real fun.

● Sometimes the scrolling doesn't keep up with the puck. Watch out for this when playing in "Arcade" mode.

Offense
Without Assists

It's entirely possible to score on a solo run, with the minimum of passing and no-one in front of the net.

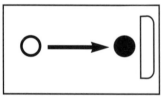

Straight Shot

Worth a try, especially on "easy" level. Usually a gift for the goalie on more difficult settings, but sometimes creeps through.

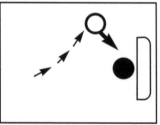

45° Shot

You can increase your chance of scoring by dribbling away from the goal, then turning and shooting at a 45° angle. Do this quickly, or the goalie covers it.

Slap Shot

Dribble very close to the net, then hit the Z button to flick the puck over the goal tender.

Turning Shot

Dribble across the face of the goal, then turn and fire at an angle.

Offense
With Assists

To really conquer this game, you need to master the art of passing, pulling the goalie out of position before slapping the puck into the net.

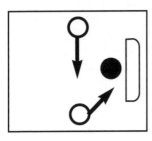

Cross Shot

The player with the puck skates toward the goal, but not directly in front of it. As he nears the net, he passes to a player on the opposite side of the ice, who plants it in the goal before the goalie can block.

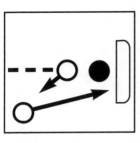

Back Pass

The player with the puck charges straight at the goal tender, when he's almost on top of him, he flicks it to a player behind him (but not directly behind). The 'minder is distracted and the second player scores.

Defense

There's no point getting 10 goals if your opponents get 12. You must learn to defend as well as shoot.

● In "Arcade" mode, without the Icing rules, you can get out of a desperate situation by shooting the puck up the rink. This is especially useful when outnumbered in front of your net, as chances are it's your player who gains control of the puck.

● Don't just charge at the man with the puck. It's sometimes better to put yourself between him and the goal, or mark an attacker, preventing a pass.

- Unless you're seriously outnumbered, keep possession and pass your way out of trouble rather than just hitting the puck. Never pass or dribble across your own goal line, though.
- If all else fails, a sly foul can seriously disrupt your opponent's attack.

Super Teams

Before you start to play, go to "Setup," then to "Options." On the Options screen, hold down the **Left** shoulder button and on the yellow "**C**" direction buttons press **Right, Left, Left, Right, Left, Left, Right, Left, Left**. The Special code 0000000001000000 appears at the foot of the screen. Four super teams (namely Williams, the 99ers, Canada, and USA) are selectable when you pick your side.

Invisible Players

During a face-off, pause the game and select "Replay" from the "Pause" options menu. Highlight a player by pressing the **Left** or **Right** shoulder button. He flashes. Press **Z**—he disappears! He's still there, but invisible!

Ads

On any setup menu (i.e. one not connected with an actual game), press the **Z** button to see an advertisement scroll across the bottom of the screen.

Ads include Campbell's Soup, Upper Deck, *Becket Hockey Monthly*, T-Mek, CCM, Chunky, Coca Cola, and Williams.

Picture Credits

From the title screen, press **A** 20 times, cycling through the stats and screens offered. You get to see the programming and development team, including a neat picture of each member.

Multi-Player Practice Mode

On the main menu, select "Practice" by pressing and holding **A**. Further players can then join in by also pressing and holding **A**, releasing the buttons when everyone's ready.

Special Codes

On an options screen, accessed before or during the game, hold any of the yellow **C** buttons and press the **Right** shoulder button. This brings up a 16-digit code at the foot of the screen. You change the digits by holding the corresponding **C** direction button (in square brackets) and pressing the **Right** shoulder button, as follows…

[D]C: First two digits.
[L]C: Digits three and four.
[U]C: Digits five and six.

Here are some crackin' codes and what they do…

Small Heads
1100000000000000
Big Heads
0100000000000000
Tiny Players
1010100000000000
Giant Players
0001010000000000
Tiny Players, Big Heads
0110010000000000

Dwarves
1000000000000000
Tiny Players, Small Heads
1110100000000000
Dwarves, Big Heads
0100100000000000
Giant Players, Small Heads
1101100000000000
Giant Players, Big Heads
0101100000000000

Super Mario 64

Course 1: Bomb World

Main floor in the castle, upstairs on the left, with blank star on door

Star 1

Climb to the very top of the mountain in this course, and you'll meet the stage boss, King Bomb, a giant black bomb with a huge mustache! Grab him from behind and throw him to the floor three times. When he is destroyed you get your first star, but knocking him off the platform or losing to him will reset the fight.

Star 2

Talk to the Koopa who hangs around near the start of this course, he'll challenge you to a race up the mountainside. The finishing line is at the very top of the mountain, win and you receive another star. The Koopa is a cheat though, so don't follow him. Just make your own way up, using the secret teleport in the mountain crevice if you want.

Star 3

From the starting point go north, here you'll find a cannon and pink bomb creatures walking around. Talk to these and they'll let you climb into the cannon and fire yourself out. Use this to blast yourself onto the floating platform directly above. Here you should find a yellow box, open this and you'll receive the third star.

Star 4

Collecting all eight of the red coins that are scattered throughout this course will earn you the forth star. Some of them are inaccessible until you've switched on the red switch palace, though. There's an explanation of this later on in this guide.

Star 5

Stand on the platform where you collected the fourth star from and then use the cannon to blast yourself at the golden coins that form circles to the north. Collect only the middle coins, and you'll receive another star.

Star 6

The huge bomb monster, who is chained to a stake in the center of this course, holds the key to the sixth star. You must avoid his attacks and use the butt bash to knock the stake he is tethered to into the ground. To show his gratitude, he removes the metal fence that guards the star.

Star 7

Finding the final star in the Bomb World is a simple matter of collecting 100 golden coins. It will simply appear wherever you collect the 100th star!

Course 2: Tower World

Main floor, on the right with a one in the star on the door

Star 1

At the very top of this course you'll find the boss of the stage, King Block. He is a giant stone slab who tries to crush you. The trick is to make him attack, then quickly move out of his way. Now, while he lies face down on the ground, use the butt bash to attack him, do this three times and he'll be destroyed. For this you get the first star.

Star 2

Once you've killed the giant stone slab boss, a new tower will be raised at the top of the mountain where he fell. It will rotate around as you climb to the top, if you manage to make it all the way up without falling to your doom, the second star will be your reward.

Star 3

Jump into the cannon on the one side of the tower and aim it forward. You should see two platforms with a flagpole running between them. Now sharpen your aim so that you're pointing directly at the flagpole itself. Blast Mario out of the cannon. If you've aimed correctly, Blast Mario directly at the pole and grab it, now climb up to collect the third star.

Star 4

Not all the stars need intricate gameplay to find them. Again in the Tower World, collecting all eight of the red coins dotted around the place will earn you another start, which will appear as you collect the last.

Star 5

Climb the tree that is found at the very start of this course. This releases an owl who offers you a lift to the top of the tower, just grab him for the lift. He flies to the top of the level and then slowly begins to lose altitude, quickly maneuver him toward the platform surrounded by a metal fence, here you'll find another star.

Star 6

Jump into the cannon, then move the sights so that you are aiming at the thin section of wall that sticks out, aim for the top corner of this. If you have aimed Mario just right, he should smash through the wall and reveal the sixth star.

Star 7

You should have been collecting all the golden coins as you go along in this world. If you've managed to round up 100 of the little dudes, you'll receive the final star for your collection.

Course 3: Water World

Main floor, upstairs on the right with a three in the star

Star 1

The first star is found in the sunken ship to the north of this course. Swim down to the ship, you'll notice a giant conger eel guards the only way. Now swim to the opposite end of the pool and then head back to the ship, the eel should have moved, uncovering the hole. At the bottom of the ship, open up the four treasure chests in this order: nearest chest, furthest chest, second nearest chest, second furthest chest. Any other combination results in an electric shock! The water now drains away, and a star is yours for the taking.

Star 2

The conger eel is again involved in the second star. The sunken ship has risen, and he can be found inside a cave deep in the ocean. Once you've located him, lure him out of his cave. You should notice that the star is attached to his tail. Use your swimming ability to move in and grab it unharmed.

Star 3

Swim into the hole that the eel was hiding in, and down the tunnel you'll find yourself in another hidden cave. At the far end of this you'll discover four treasure chests. Open the one closest to you first, next open the chest to your right, now the chest to the left, and finally the chest furthest away from you. This yields another star.

Star 4

For another golden star, you must be a thorough collector again. Collect all eight of the red coins scattered throughout this course inside clams and you'll be handsomely rewarded.

Star 5

Jump into the cannon located at the start of this world. Now aim yourself at the stone spire to the north—your aim must be precise. If your aim is true, Mario should grab the spire as he flies past. Drop down onto the small ledge below, and collect the star.

Star 6

The sixth golden star is positioned over an iron vent near the sunken ship wreck. Mario won't be able to go anywhere near it in his normal mode, but collecting the power-up from the green box on the edge of the pool will turn him into a metallic superhero. Now he'll be heavy enough to float through the current and collect the star.

Star 7

The final star in the Water World can be found by collecting 100 golden coins from all around the place. The star will appear when you pick up the last one.

Course 4: Snow World

Main floor, on the left with a three on the door

Star 1

At the start of the world you'll notice a log cabin. Jump down the chimney and you'll find yourself at the start of a large snow slide—yup, you've got to survive the slide, controlling Mario as he goes. Make it to the bottom safely, and you'll be rewarded with a star.

Star 2

Near the log cabin at the start of this course, you'll find a baby penguin. Pick him up and either carry him all the way down to the bottom of the mountain or take the slide once more, with the penguin sitting in your lap for the ride. When you reach the bottom you'll find his mother, she'll reward you with the second star.

Star 3

Once you've returned the baby penguin to his mother, use the chimney to enter the log cabin at the start of the course. Once again, mother penguin will be waiting for you and will challenge you to a race. If you win, chat to her and she'll give you your prize—another star!

Star 4

Collect all eight of the red coins scattered throughout the course, and you'll receive another star, but they're now becoming more difficult to find. Make sure you check behind every object, and in every corner of the world, and you'll find them, no problem!

Star 5

At the top of the mountain you'll find a snowball, as you approach it'll start rolling down the hill. You must make it

to the snowman's head, found half way down the mountain, before the snowball does—however you can't use any short cuts. If you succeed, the two snowballs will join and form a giant snowman, talk to him and you'll receive a star.

Star 6

Jump into the cannon that is found close to the mother penguin. Now aim the cannon at the tree to the west (use the picture for added accuracy), Mario should grab hold of the tree if your aim is true. Now follow this platform until you find the sixth star!

Star 7

Guess where the last star is hiding out? In the golden coins around the world of course! Collect 100 golden coins and you'll receive the final star.

Course 5: Haunted Mansion

Main floor, either door with no stars, down hall past ghost, into garden and hit large ghost

Star 1

In the main hall of the mansion you'll be confronted by a group of small ghosts called Baby Boos. Kill about four and a large ghost, Big Boo, will appear. Kill him and you've got your first star.

Star 2

Enter the small house, it's opposite the main mansion, and follow its path until you come to a carousel. Here you must kill a bunch of small ghosts, then the big one that appears again—if you survive the wrath of the Boos, you'll receive a star.

Star 3

In the main mansion go upstairs and search the rooms until you find the library. In here you'll find a bookcase with three books sticking out. Push the middle one first, then the book on the right, and finally the book to your left. A secret door opens revealing the third star.

Star 4

There are more red coins scattered inside the ghost house, collect eight and again you'll be blessed with a star.

Star 5

From the main hall go up stairs and through the door to your right. In this room jump up onto the platform in the corner and look up. You'll see a hidden platform, use a back-flip to jump up onto it. You are now in the attic, from here go through the main double doors and kill the Big Boo ghost—a star will appear on the roof. You must use precise jumping skills to climb across the sloped roof and collect it.

Star 6

For this star you must have activated the Blue Switch Palace. Go up onto the upper balcony of the main hall and use the blue cube—this turns Mario partially invisible. Quickly dash up to the attic, to the left you should see a painting of a blue ghost, now walk straight through! Here you'll find an eye monster, kill it and collect the sixth star!

Star 7

Collecting all 100 golden coins in the Haunted Mansion will earn Mario the seventh and final star.

Course 6: Cavern World

Lower floor, from fire picture go right and through door with star

Star 1

Go right from the start, walk past the orange spiders and the leaping flames. Then through the door and slide down the pole. Next you'll come to some gray stairs, follow the arrows to reach a floating platform and some red coins. Pick these up, then leap off to a ledge with a pole. Climb this to reach another platform, where you'll find your first star.

Star 2

Go back through the tunnel, take the elevator, go through the doors and left. You'll see two boulders rolling towards you. Run up and you will be in a room with a caged star. The elevator will take you back to an underground lake, where you'll find Nessie. Leap onto him, and he'll take you to the second star.

Star 3

Use the metallic suit and then drop Mario into the water. Follow the pathway to the purple switch, hit this to open the barriers on the double door, and enter. Use a long jump to reach the third star.

Star 4

From the start, go left. There's a green ledge near a dip in the ground, back flip onto this and enter the room. Take the elevator to the forth star in this world.

Star 5

Now roam around and find the gray ledge. Back flip onto it and you'll find yourself above the rolling boulders and see an apparently unreachable star. Get up onto the red bars and leap off the sign, climbing over to reach the fifth star.

Star 6

Just past the rolling boulder section you'll find a star up on a high ledge between two walls. Bounce from wall to wall and the star will be easy to reach.

Star 7

Finally, 100 stars can be collected to give yourself the seventh star.

Course 7: Fire World

Lower floor in castle with fire picture

Star 1

From the start point head to the opposite side of the course, here you'll find a platform that is guarded by a giant Viking bomb. Knock him into the lava and a staircase will rise, leading to the star. Climb this, and the platforms fall away, but you'll be able to pick the star up from here.

Star 2

Not far from the point where the first star was collected. You'll find another platform. This one is guarded by three small Viking bombs—knock them all into the lava. With this done another giant Viking bomb will appear, do the same to him, and receive the star.

Star 3

In the corner of the course you'll notice that a group of platforms are protected by a metal fence. You must use the platforms to maneuver Mario around into this area. Use the spinning log, by running in the opposite direction to the way you want to move, to get across the lava, and collect the star.

Star 4

You'll find another eight red coins in this course, they're all on Bowser's sliding block puzzle. Collect them all, and you'll receive another star for your troubles.

Star 5

Jump into the volcano that is found in the center of this course. Once inside use the platforms that are arranged around the edge of the volcano to make your way upward, a star is your reward.

Star 6

To get this star you must once again jump into the volcano. This time jump aboard the moving platform to the east. As this winds its way upward, you must perform a number of tricky jumps. The sixth star awaits you at the top.

Star 7

As in all the other worlds in *Super Mario 64*, collecting 100 golden coins will make the seventh and last star appear. Now just pick it up!

Course 8: Desert World

Lower floor, left from fire picture to dead end. Through wall

Star 1

Collect 100 golden coins and you'll receive a star. 65 are outside the pyramid and 40 inside, including five special ones which count toward the total, make sure you've collected all the outside ones before you enter because there's no going back!

Star 2

The second star is in the hands (or should that be claws?) of an annoying vulture who swoops around in the sky. You must use one of the red and orange brick towers to get close to the bird. Now jump up and grab it as he flies past.

Star 3

This star is found at the very top of the pyramid in a small hole. You must use a ledge that runs around the outside of the ancient monument to get it. Take care, as the ledge gets progressively thinner the higher you go!

Star 4

Inside the pyramid you should notice a red and orange brick building in the center. Use the platforms around the side to climb up until you have enough height to jump onto this small building. You must now drop off the edge and maneuver Mario so that he grabs onto the ledge below before he hits the ground. This is VERY difficult. Once inside, you must defeat the Hands Boss, his weak points are his blue eyes; they are only vulnerable for a few seconds, so timing is crucial. Do this, and you'll receive a well earned fourth star!

Star 5

The eight red coins to be picked up for the fifth star are sprinkled everywhere. You can pick up four by using the flying cap and circling around in the air. The rest are found around the world, one right at the start.

Star 6

This sixth star is found inside the pyramid itself. It's time to climb up the thin ledge once again. Just before you reach the top there'll be a flower monster to kill. Dispose of him, then crawl the rest of the way to the top. If you're careful you'll make it, and the star will be there waiting for you.

Star 7

Inside the pyramid five special gold coins can be found. You must collect all of these to receive the final star. They are suspended on platforms found at the very top of the pyramid, so your jumping ability is in for a rigorous test before you can reach them all!

Course 9: Submarine World

Lower floor, through the large star door

Star 1

Jump straight into the water and swim down and through the corridors. Eventually you'll reach Bowser's submarine floating in the ocean cavern. Jump on the purple switch to activate the gangway. This will lead you onto the sub where a star will be waiting.

Star 2

On the far side of the water are two power-up blocks separated by grates. The first one will be a Pixel Mario icon that will make our hero transparent, the second will be the Metallic Mario icon to make the guy heavier. Collect them both, then head for the bottom of the ocean. Now walk over to the grating above the star to collect it.

Star 3

If you swim down to the whirlpool, you'll find four treasure chests. These must be opened in the correct sequence to yield another star. With the clam to the north-east of you, collect the chest to the north, then the one to the south-west, then the one in between these two, then finally the one slightly to the south-east. A star will be born!

Star 4

Pressing the purple switch will also make a staircase appear. You can now reach a set of yellow and black poles. Ride on these to collect all eight of the red coins. Now you'll have another star!

Star 5

The whirlpool under the submarine in the first area will produce a circle of water rings. Swim through all of these and you'll earn yourself the fifth star.

Star 6

The manta-ray in the first area will also produce a circle of water rings. Collect all of these and the sixth star will be yours!

Star 7

Collect the 100 golden coins dotted around for the last star. The last five of these are underneath the black hole in the water. Swim very carefully when collecting these or you'll be sucked in.

Course 10: Snowman World

Upper floor, in room with mirror. The entrance can be seen in the mirror

Star 1

Jump over the waves in the snowy platform using Mario's double jumping ability, then you'll start your climb up the snowman building. Run around the wooden platforms, then use the penguin to shield Mario from the snowman's breath. Cross the bridge and a star will be waiting.

Star 2

Just before the snow wave machine, you'll find a blue spiked cannonball dude. You need to push him off his icy platform, or get in the way so he slides off by himself. This will give you the second star in this snowy world.

Star 3

If you look closely at the massive ice cube near the start of the world, you'll see that it's really a 3D maze. There's an entrance around the back; just back flip up to the top level and drop down to where the star is located. There's only one way to reach it, so get it right.

Star 4

Near the snow wave machine, there's a wooden platform leading across the water. To get onto this, wait for the snowball head monster to emerge from the water, then butt-bounce him to send Mario spinning through the air. He should reach the platform where he'll find a yellow box containing the star.

Star 5

Also on this wooden platform will be four of the eight red coins you must collect for another star. The box here contains a turtle shell. Use this to surf over the ice and under the cannonball monster to another two red coins. Once eight are collected, the star will be yours.

Star 6

The turtle shell will also allow Mario to surf up the almost vertical pathway near the snow wave machine. Up the top there's an igloo containing a Pixel Mario power-up. Collect this and a star will be easy pickings.

Star 7

Collecting 100 gold coin points will give you the last star, but beware! Some of the coins dotted around will change into little green creatures when you go near. You can't kill these, so take is easy!

Course 11: Water Puzzle World

Upper floor of castle with spider picture

Star 1

There's a yellow ! box near the bottom of the world. To reach it you've got to hit the switch and raise the water level so that Mario is within reach. Now just amble over and hit the box for your first star.

Star 2

Another of these ! blocks can be found at the top of the world. The water must be raised to its maximum height before Mario can get near to it. When it has risen, make the little guy walk the plank and the star will be yours.

Star 3

Hitting the yellow star boxes or moving the white and red boxes around the world uncovers five secret spots. Once you've discovered all five of these, a third star will fall out of the sky to be collected.

Star 4

Raise the water to the highest level and perform a double jump from the wooden platform. You should aim for the checked platform where you'll find a pink cannonball guy who'll activate a cannon for you. Using this you can fire Mario to a corner cage brimming with red coins. Collect all eight of the red coins and you'll receive the fourth star.

Star 5

Right at the top of this world you'll find a purple switch. Hit this to get onto a cage. Now ride the wooden platform down, you'll need to jump to start this thing moving. If you've already destroyed the wooden box, there will be a hole in the base of the cage where you can enter. Now jump on the platform as it rises. Your fifth star should be waiting at the top.

Star 6

Time to get into the cannon once again, this time to aim Mario at the very top of the world. There's a star hanging out in the rafters; you've just got to seek it out and fire. A couple of attempts should safely bag this one.

Star 7

Believe it or not, the final star in the Water Puzzle World comes along when you've collected 100 golden coins from all around the place.

Course 12: Mushroom World

Upper floor of castle with mushroom picture

Star 1

The first star is where you'd expect it to be—right at the very top of the mountain. Just take your time and walk Mario to the top. The star will be just sat, waiting to be picked up.

Star 2

When you've reached the top of the mountain, you'll encounter a monkey. If you've already played with the first monkey, found down on the base of the level—losing your cap to him, then recovering it again—this one will lead Mario off to the second star.

Star 3

The eight red coins in this world are divided up between the mushrooms near the base of the mountain and on the platforms near the nasty moles. Collect them all for the third star.

Star 4

Right at the very top of the mountain, roam around until you find a blank wall. Finding a wall like this is always suspicious in a Mario game, and if you jump through it you'll discover a secret slide. Make it to the bottom of the slide and a star will be waiting for you.

Star 5

Everything seems to take place at the top of the mountain. Make your way up there again, and this time look for the purple switch. Hitting this makes a temporary platform appear. By walking onto this and jumping up you can grab star number five.

Star 6

Pick up 100 of those lovely golden coins found scattered throughout the world for another shiny star.

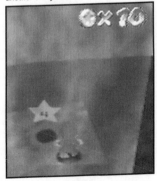

Star 7

The final star is resting on a mushroom near the start of the world, but it is almost impossible to collect it by leaping. Instead, talk to the pink cannonball to activate a secret cannon. To reach the cannon, jump on the mushroom with the blue coin, twist around the viewpoint so that you can make out a narrow ledge down below. Leap onto this, following it around to the cannon. Hit the star and you succeed in this level: miss and you're dead!

Course 13: Green Pipe World

Upper floor through door with star

Star 1

Another mountain walk is in store for the first star. Make Mario tiny, and just walk up to the top where the first star can be picked up.

Star 2

When Mario is large, there are five special areas that he must walk through to be awarded the second star. The cannon, the beach doorway, the wooden plank near the entrance to the mountain, the top of the mountain, and the place where the cannonballs appear. Visit them all, and the star is yours.

Star 3

Keep your eyes peeled for the eight red coins once again in this world. Pick them all up on your travels and the third star will be yours.

Star 4

Back at the start of the world, go left and across a set of platforms. Here you'll be attacked by five Venus fly traps, one after the other. Punch all five successfully, and the fourth star will be in your hands.

Star 5

The fifth star is earned by racing a Koopa Turtle found just past the hole where the cannonballs run out. The finish point is the flag in the corner of the world. Just get there before him as small Mario, and the star is yours.

Star 6

Visit the very top of the mountain when large and butt-bounce it twice to start the water draining away. A hole will appear, just big enough for the small Mario to squeeze through. Use the nearby pipe to transform and enter the hole. Down below you'll encounter a caterpillar. Pick a fight with him, and win the sixth star.

Star 7

Finally, don't forget to collect the 100 gold coin points littered around the world for this last star.

Course 14: Clockwork World

Upper floor, up stairs to the top, in door with huge star

Star 1

When the clock has stopped, follow the route past the face and use the meshing gears to take Mario to a cage with a conveyor belt alongside it. The first star is inside the cage. Just run over and grab it!

Star 2

Make your way back to where you found the first star, but this time backflip up onto the top of the cage and keep moving upward. Jump from the platform with the purple clockwork mousetrap on it, but be careful—the gaps in the platform can't be seen from all angles. Make your way carefully to the star and pick it up.

Star 3

Get the clock moving again. This time position Mario on the hour hand as it rotates around. This will take Mario near to a star hanging out in a small alcove. Use a diving leap to grab the star before Mario drops.

Star 4

Again with the clock moving, position Mario on the very tip of the clock hand and jump when you see the ledge coming up at the very top of the world. Here you'll find a blue coin box, butt bounce this, and the star will drop out for collection.

Star 5

The eight red coins in the Clockwork World are near the start, with spinning clock pieces as platforms underneath them. It's best to stop the clock to pick these up. Use back-flips to carefully pick them off, one by one.

Star 6

Star number six is right at the top of the clock once again, so start climbing. It's inside a cage and tricky to reach. The best way is to jump onto the top of the cage, then wait for the platform to move in and underneath it. Jump onto the platform, and the star will be yours.

Star 7

Predictably, the seventh and final star for the Clockwork World can be earned by collecting all 100 gold coin points from around the place.

Course 15: Magic Carpet World

Upper floor in room containing courses 14 and 15, jump from platform in corner

Star 1

The first thing you'll need to find in the Magic Carpet World is the giant floating ship overhead—you can't really miss it! It's reminiscent of the sunken ship in Water World, and all you've got to do is make your way over to it and grab the star.

Star 2

Now take the magic carpet and go as high as possible into the air. You'll eventually come across a floating building with a green roof. There's a star on the roof, so grab it as you go past.

Star 3

From the very start of this world, move forward from the first rotating platform, and you'll arrive at a gray building. This contains all the red coins you could possibly want. Collect the eight, and the third star is yours.

Star 4

Moving left from the rotating platform in star three will take Mario over a set of swings and onto stony pyramid objects. There's a purple switch here that will make it slightly easier to grab the star.

Star 5

Back at the floating ship you'll find a cannon, so you know you're going to have to go for a ride. Shoot Mario out of this and onto the floating island high in the sky. The fifth star is here, to collect it quick!

Star 6

Back to the rotating platforms again! This time move Mario toward the tilting bridges and the swinging platforms. Climb up the steep wooden slope and across the swinging platform, and you should see the star on the end.

Star 7

To finish the Magic Carpet World off, pick up all 100 gold coin points and grab the final star.

The final 15 stars

Star 1

In the main floor of the castle, go up the stairs and there will be a door on your right with a star on it. In the small room there will be pictures of the Princess. Jump through the one on the right and finish the race for a star.

Star 2

In the room with the picture of course three, there are two holes just above that can be jumped into. One holds an extra life and the other a bonus swimming level, with eight red coins to collect for a star.

Star 3

Once 20 stars have been collected, you must attempt to catch the bunny in the lower level of the castle, near courses six through eight. Run and press punch to dive on him—he's not the easiest rabbit to grab! Succeed, and a star is yours.

Star 4

Again, after collecting 20 stars, talk to Toad in the room containing the entrance to course six. He will give you a star without you having to do anything!

Star 5

Collect 50 stars and return to the basement of the castle to find the bunny again. He just doesn't know when to stay away—grab him, and your star will appear.

Star 6

After collecting the 50 stars, move up to the upper level of the castle, where courses 10 through 13 are located. Talk to Toad (the toadstool guy), and he'll give you another star.

Star 7

Toad appears again in the room containing courses 14 and 15. Chat with him once more, and he'll give you yet another star for your collection.

Star 8

Near the entrance to course 15 there's a bonus room high up on the wall. Collect all the red coins in here for another star.

Star 9

Collecting all eight red coins from Bowser World One will provide you with the ninth extra star in *Super Mario 64*.

Star 10

There are another eight red coins to be collected from Bowser World Two for your tenth extra star.

Star 11

Wait for it... Bowser World Three has yet another eight red coins to be collected for star 11.

Star 12

Visit the Green Switch Palace and collect all eight of the red coins in there for another star.

Star 13

Pay a visit to the Blue Switch Palace, and there will be another eight red coins to be collected for a star.

Star 14

The Red Switch Palace has the final eight red coins to be collected—yielding the fourteenth star.

Star 15

One hundred nineteen collected... one to go! This final star is in the same location as star one—at the picture of the Princess on the main castle floor. Finish the race in under 21 seconds, and the star is yours.

Bowser World One

You can find the first Bowser encounter on the main floor of the castle. Just go up the stairs and through the trapdoor with the huge star on it. To kill the big brute, just run around him, pick him up by his tail, and rotate the joystick to spin him around. The faster you spin, the further he'll fly when you let go. All you've got to do now is send him flying off into a bomb and he'll be finished. Your prize for seeing off Bowser will be the key to open up the lower floor in the castle.

Bowser World Two

This Bowser lair is found on the lower floor of the castle. Again, go through the door with the huge star on it to find him. He's killed in exactly the same way as before, by spinning him around and letting go when he's perfectly lined up with a bomb. This time your prize will be the key to the upper floor of the castle. You can't access all the courses up there immediately, though—you'll still need to collect the right number of stars first.

Bowser World Three

This third and final Bowser-bashing experience is found on the upper floor of the castle. Go through the star door and up the staircase. If you haven't collected enough stars, the stairs will go on forever, but if you have enough, you'll get to the end and meet Bowser again.

This one's similar to the first two lairs, but this time you'll have to throw Bowser into the bombs three times to kill him. To get to the monster, you'll have to overcome tons of challenges, but they're all things that have cropped up before in the game. Just use all your techniques to reach his lair.

After throwing Bowser into the bomb the first two times, the platform you're standing on will change into the shape of a star. This will make things slightly more tricky for the final bombing.

Your prize here is finishing the game—that can't be bad!

PilotWings 64

This aerial outing was one of the first games ever released for the N64. With three different aircrafts to fly as well as bonus games to win, you won't beat this game in a day...

Gyrocopter Missions
Mission One: Lake Island

Head for the first hoop. As you travel through, the sphere beyond turns into a hoop. Fly through this, and the third hoop is created. Fly through and then land, keeping as close to the center of the runway as possible. Points are gained for accurate, smooth landings and lost through hitting the ground too hard at too high a speed, or by landing too far from or not aligned with the dotted line.

Mission Two,
Stage One: Crescent Island

More hoops to fly through. Look out for the one in a hole at the top of the mountain. This is the only difficult hoop to hit— your real enemy here is the time limit. Accelerate as much as possible, but make sure you hit the hoop on your first try.

Mission Two,
Stage Two: Crescent Island

This one isn't too difficult. Using your missiles, shoot three targets and return to base. Be fast for maximum points. Aiming is easier if you switch to first-person perspective.

Mission Three,
Stage One: USA Island

Another hoops stage. Unlike in earlier outings, though, not every hoop is obviously placed. Look under bridges for the hidden ones. Each covers at least two circles, but the white ones are bonuses, and not essential. These, as always, offer more points. An accurate landing is more important than a good time on this stage, but be as quick as you can.

Mission Three,
Stage Two: USA Island

More blasting. The targets are fairly well scattered, so work out a sensible route to save time. Landing is tricky here, as the runway is surrounded by obstacles. Follow the road in.

Mission Three,
Stage Three: USA Island

This mission has an enemy that fights back: a stone slab-throwing creature who won't stand still and be shot. Hit him five times to win. Each time you score a hit he runs forward, so don't get in too close. The slabs he throws at you can also be shot. Finish in 150 seconds for maximum points.

Mission Four,
Stage One: Icy Island

Back to hoops! Watch out for hoops inside other hoops, half buried hoops (usually white bonus ones), and drastic variations in height. Some rotate, too—use your speed to time these fly-throughs accurately.

There's a nightmare head-wind, so careful flying is essential. Hitting the regular hoops opens the white bonus ones—flying through these offers more points than the blue efforts.

Mission Four,
Stage Two: Icy Island

This stage is full of floating spheres, tastefully decorated in blue and white stripes. Shoot or fly through 20 of these to complete the stage. It's better to fly slowly and hit the targets more often than to speed through and miss.

Mission Four,
Stage Three: Icy Island

Another encounter with old stony face. This time he throws ice blocks and swims for cover. Use the same tactics as before—find him, blast him, and get away. Fly low.

Rocket Pack Missions
Mission One: Lake Island

Just lift off, fly through the orange sphere as close to the center as possible, and land. Points are awarded for flying close to the middle of the sphere, and for making a soft, slow landing in the center of the bullseye on the target zone.

Mission Two, Stage One:
USA Island

Collect the yellow rings for points. Also, red rings appear from time to time, but they don't last long. For bonus points, fly through before the clock in the center of the ring counts down for bonus points. The red rings usually appear between skyscrapers, under bridges and in other hard-to-reach places.

Mission Two, Stage Two: USA Island

This stage initially features a floating pad and an apparently-pointless orange and white sphere. Landing on the floating pad turns one of the spheres into another pad, as well as boosts your fuel—careful, some of the pads move around. Take off again and the pad disappears. Land on each pad in turn, there are five in all. A fast speed gives more points.

Mission Three, Stage One: Icy Island

Hit the two blue spheres as close to the center as possible. They split into orange spheres which must be collected. The blue spheres are found over the port and near the broken ice. A fast speed and a soft landing are important.

Mission Three, Stage Two: Icy Island

Fly through the yellow rings. Sometimes flying through a ring turns the next one red. Fly through this before the timer in the center runs down, or suffer a time penalty.

Mission Three,
Stage Three: Icy Island

Another speed mission. Push the green sphere found near the igloo into the green and blue pillar as quickly as possible, then land—softly and in the center of the target, as always. Aim for a time of around 75 seconds.

Mission Four,
Stage One: Crescent Island

Time is the most important factor here. You start outside a tunnel. Fly in and pick your way through its twists and turns, including several vertical sections, before reaching the exit. Hit the walls and you suffer point penalties.

Use the **Z** button to stabilize your flight if heading for grief. Watch out for some dodgy polygon updates when the corridor narrows.

Mission Four,
Stage Two: Crescent Island

Again, you must guide the green sphere into the green and blue column. Rolling it along the floor can be hazardous—it usually gets stuck en route. Keep it in the air.

Mission Four,
Stage Three: Crescent Island

This is another stage where you must fly from one floating platform to another. Careful not to hit the rocks or land too heavily.

Hang Glider Missions
Mission One: Lake Island

This one's not too difficult, just a simple glide through three rings. Use this mission to practice your landings.

Mission Two,
Stage One: Icy Island

Follow the radar to the smoke stack or chimney. Take a snapshot of it and head for home. If your picture turns out ok, you get a message.

Mission Two,
Stage Two: Icy Island

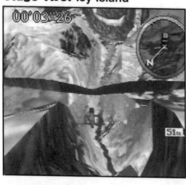

You start the mission on top of a mountain, far higher than the hoops through which you must fly. As soon as you take off, dive sharply. Fly through as many hoops as is possible, then climb, bank left, and land on the target. Good luck!

Mission Three,
Stage One: Crescent Island

Use the thermals to rise—aim to climb around 100 meters in each, staying within the thermal for as long as possible. When you reach 400 meters, you're given a message. Land as quickly as possible for increased points.

Mission Three,
Stage Two: Crescent Island

A photography mission. Find and photograph the whale and the fountain, then cruise in to land on the target.

Mission Three,
Stage Three: Crescent Island

Stay in the air for three minutes—you get a message. Land as soon after that as is possible. Ideally, you should time your landing so the message appears a second before you touch down. This gives maximum points.

Mission Four,
Stage One: USA Island

This is a height mission. Climb as high as possible on the thermals before the four-minute timer expires. Six hundred meters is a good target. Again, stay in the thermals as long as is possible and leave them heading for the next ones.

Mission Four,
Stage Two: USA Island

More rings to fly through! Wing your way through eight of them before landing. To achieve a respectable score you must be quick—find the fastest route and stick to it.

Mission Four,
Stage Three: USA Island

This time your photographic subjects are the space shuttle, a sea monster and a cruise ship. The image should be in the center of the picture, covering as much of it as is possible without spilling over the edge and cutting bits off.

Bonus Stages

If you complete missions with all three crafts and earn a silver crest or higher (averaging 80% on each stage), you get to play a bonus game. The Bird Man is an exception; here you need gold licenses. These are as follows…

Mission One: Bird Man
Mission Two: Cannonball
Mission Three: Skydiving
Mission Four: Jumble-Hopper

Bird Man

This isn't so much a bonus stage as a neat way of exploring an already-completed level. Finish an island with gold licenses for all three crafts and you can fly around the respective land, taking photographs at whim.

There are no mission objectives, no points and the Bird Man is extremely easy to fly; it's really just a simple means of exploring a fully-conquered island. You can land anywhere you choose, but you can't walk along the ground. Like the regular craft, if you crash too hard you're killed.

Cannonball

No prizes for guessing what to do here—aim your aeronaut bang on the bullseye. You adjust the elevation and direction of your cannon. The power meter rises and falls of its own accord. Hit the button to select the currently displayed value. You can't steer your character in flight, so your chosen trajectory needs to be dead-on. The own-eye view is more useful than the "chase" viewpoint, offering cross-hairs with which to aim and leaving the screen uncluttered.

There are three missions on offer, with four individual targets per mission. You get three shots at each target, with only the highest counting towards your mission total. A bullseye gets you 25 points.

The key to achieving a high score is consistency—use the same power rating for each shot, adjusting elevation and direction to compensate for inaccuracies. It's best to use full power as this is easier to reproduce in subsequent shots. Full power lessens the effects of wind, too. Also, the sooner you get a shot on the target board the more time you have to refine your aim and get the highest score. Try to make sure your first blast finds its mark.

Skydiving

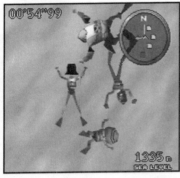

Skydiving is about as easy as throwing yourself out of an airplane. Each of the three missions consists of a single dive, during which you must perform five tricks and land. Using the **A** button and the joystick, draw level with your three colleagues. When you do so, they take formation and a yellow outline of your character appears in your place. Draw your skydiver into this position—when successful, a timer counts down three seconds and you get the ok message indicating a successful trick. For the maximum 50 points, you must complete five tricks before hitting the clouds.

Once through the cloud layer you must land on the target. Hold freefall for as long as you dare, as a fast mission offers more points. When your parachute is open forward movement is automatic; the only control you have over your descent is speed (the **A** button) and rotation (left or right on the joystick). The closer to the bullseye you land, the better. Hold the **A** button to make sure you're in the correct posture as your feet hit the ground. For maximum points, freefall to 150m, press and hold **A** to slow your descent, open your chute below 100m and hit the target on landing.

Jumble-Hopper

The object of this bonus game is as straightforward as they come—just get to the exit. Your mighty boots send you leaping into the air, with the **A** button offering a powerful jump and the **B** button a less powerful one. Holding the joystick forward focuses your energy on distance, while holding it back concentrates power on height.

When you land, you have a limited time to set the angle and direction of your next jump, so be quick. A fast mission scores most points, but you lose them for hitting the water.

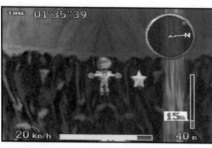

Cheats and Secrets

● There's a cool secret to be found on Icy Island. Fly into the cave as shown (the Rocket Pack works best), work your way into the cavern, and fly down through the hole in the floor. You enter a chamber containing a star as seen here. Collect it and you reappear outside the cave—as Bird Man.

● Fly into the cave found under the castle on Lake Island. It's blocked by a steel grid. When you fly out again, it's night! The trip must have taken longer than you thought....

● Under the stone bridge seen on the edge of Lake Island directly opposite the fair is a star. Fly into it to become Bird Man, soaring high over Lake Island.

● On mission One, Stage One of the cannonball bonus game, try aiming the cannon at Mario's head on Mount Rushmore. Hit it and he turns into Wario. If you hit it a second time, it turns back into Mario. Wow! A completely useless inclusion, but one that's well worth checking out.